TARGET PRACTICE

TARGET PRACTICE

Nicholas Meyer

 Harcourt Brace Jovanovich, Inc., New York

The characters in this book are purely imaginary,
bearing no relation to actual people, living or dead,
except by coincidence.

Library of Congress Cataloging in Publication Data

Meyer, Nicholas.
    Target practice.

    I. Title.
PZ4.M6135Tar ₍PS3563.F88₎   813'.5'4   73-19959
ISBN 0-15-187997-4

B C D E

For my father

TARGET PRACTICE

1 It was after midnight when I boarded the plane and I was tired. It wasn't just the trial, though they can be enervating enough when you're waiting around to give your testimony and then sticking to your motel room in case someone wants to call you back to the stand. I knew practically nobody in Washington, and the city was jumping with too many problems of its own to pay attention to me. It was funny to think that I was one of a handful of people in town who were there for a trial unconnected with Watergate. But that feeling of happy distinction grew boring quite shortly. When I knew I wasn't wanted at court, I made the rounds of the tourist attractions, the monuments, the statues, cherry blossoms, and tablets erected to memorialize the land of the free and the home of the brave. I almost phoned a cousin of mine a couple of times in the evenings, but I'd never liked him, and I always backed off with my finger in the dial.

Once the trial was over they weren't paying my motel bill any more, so it was time to leave. And American

3

was offering 20 per cent off if you flew at night, which explains why I was so tired when I boarded the 12:40 707 from Dulles for LA International. On the way out in the cab, I had fantasized that nobody much would be flying at such an ungodly hour and imagined a kindly stewardess removing the armrests and letting me stretch out the way I'd seen Bill Russell do in the ads.

No such luck. I had no idea the economy was in such terrible shape until I saw the horde of late-night travelers whose budgets must have been about that of a down-at-heel private eye. And then there was all that funny business of getting X-rayed for hidden weapons before they let you board. The machine didn't catch anybody but it sure as hell slowed everything down. By this time I was practically walking in my sleep and unconcerned with highjackers. I just wanted a seat with a window so that I could prop myself against something. This would enable me to sleep during the highjacking. There were lots of students piling on in front of me. I hoped they didn't plan on singing Boola-Boola or civil rights songs or whatever college students were singing that year.

I got my seat by the window and asked for a pillow. Before the seat next to me was filled, I'd switched off the overhead light and fallen asleep. My dreams were confused—they always are—and I was aware of a wailing somewhere outside my window in the indigo night. I don't know how long I'd been out when an air pocket jarred my head loose from the pillow and the pillow slid down to the armrest, letting me bang myself awake against the fuselage. The place was almost totally dark, with just little pin points of light here and there up ahead, indicating insomniacs and night owls with their late-night diversions. The only sound was a reassuring hum of engines and some distant laughter from the stewardesses' pantry. The girls were used to it.

I wasn't really awake. Somewhere the wailing from my dream was still going on, besides the hum. It took me quite some time to realize this. I had started to turn on the overhead light, but couldn't muster the energy for the reach. Instead, I fished out a cigarette and lit up.

The wailing wasn't really wailing; it was more a sort of sniffling cough. And it wasn't off to my right. It was coming from the seat next to me on my left. I twisted around for a look, but it was too dark to see.

"Is this smoke bothering you?" It wasn't the right question, of course. The sounds had been going before I lit up.

"No, that's all right." This was followed by another sniffle.

"You're sure?"

"Yes." Another sniffle. Whoever it was didn't have a handkerchief.

"Here." I stubbed out my cigarette and handed over a packet of Kleenex.

She took it with murmured thanks and said something about having used hers all up.

"Is anything wrong? Can I get you anything else?"

"No, really."

All right, I thought to myself. I scrunched back to face the window and tucked my pillow into place again. But it wasn't any good; you can't just drift off to sleep when someone in the chair next to you is crying her eyes out—and blowing her nose. I was wondering what the occupant of the seat on the other side of the wailer was making of all this and turned to look. It was dark, but not so dark that I couldn't see the seat was empty. So it hadn't been a sellout flight after all. And the wailer hadn't thought to move into the empty seat and leave some space of silence between us.

I pulled out another cigarette, lit it, and studied the wailer for a few seconds by the light of my match. She was sitting with her legs propped up in front of her, was resting her arms on her knees, and had buried her head in her arms. Altogether not too profitable a glimpse. But she had good legs and she wore what looked like good shoes. Her blonde hair was tied in a bun and she had one of those Pucci scarves tied in a bow in it. I sensed rather than saw a dark pleated skirt pulled demurely—but barely—over the tops of her knees.

"Look, something's on your mind. Why don't you tell me about it—or talk about anything else, if you'd care to, instead. I'd be happy to listen," I lied. "I'm a great listener," I said truthfully.

"Thanks. I don't want to talk to anyone just now." This after a pause. My match was out but her voice was muffled. Her head was still in her arms.

"Yes you do—or you would've moved over to that empty seat and let me get some sleep."

"What?" In the black, her head came up in sharp surprise, looked in my direction, and then twisted around to examine the empty seat. "Well, you're wrong. As it happens, I didn't realize the seat was empty. I'll move now if you like."

She gathered herself for the effort but I held out a restraining arm.

"That's okay. I'm wide awake now." Too true.

"Please let go of my arm."

"Sorry. All I meant was it's okay." She was probably

as pretty as she smelled, and used to being mauled. "But if you didn't notice the empty seat then you're in even worse shape than I thought. Are you sure you don't want a shoulder to cry on? I'm really not doing anything more important."

There was a silence while she considered this.

"What's your name?"

"Mark Brill. What's yours?"

"Mark." She tested it. "Were you named for someone in your family?"

"Mark was my father's favorite Gospel. Maybe he got carried away. Who're you named for?"

"Nobody," she replied with a dismal relapse. "I'm just Shelly Rollins. Shelly Bettina Rollins," she added, after thinking about it.

"Why are you crying, Shelly?"

"I've been trying not to," she protested, using another of my Kleenexes.

"I know you have, but what's the trouble?"

She hesitated a moment longer.

"My brother's dead." And she started to cry some more. I felt we were on close enough footing and slipped an arm behind her shoulders. She didn't resist, and I let her sob some against my jacket. It was Harris tweed, and after eight years it could take just about anything.

"Were you close?"

Underneath my arm she gave a half-hearted shrug.

"Not really, I guess. Maybe that's why I feel so bad now."

"Was his death sudden?"

"I guess you could say so." She gave a choked laugh. "He shot himself."

Suddenly we were both sitting very still. In the darkness, the hum of the engines came up again in our ears. Up ahead I noticed that the last of the lights had been extinguished. Except for the crew we were the only ones awake, yet it seemed, too, as though the whole plane were listening. I flicked some ash from my cigarette into where I thought my ashtray was and wished I hadn't begun this conversation.

"You're on your way home?"

She nodded against my tweed. I wondered how many other plane passengers were sitting alone at this odd hour whizzing across the country to attend funerals. I wondered what to say to her. I said I was sorry.

"It's all their fault. If they hadn't started in with their charges, this never would have happened."

"Whose fault?"

"The Army's—and Major Bruno's. As if four years in prison camp weren't enough." She sat up abruptly and reached for the overhead light. "Don't look at me."

"I'm not." I couldn't if I wanted to, the shock of the light was so great. I sat and let my retinas get used to the idea beneath closed lids while I listened to her unclasping her purse and fiddling around with her make-up.

"Your brother was—?"

"Sergeant Harold Rollins, that's right." She blew her nose with finality. "Harold Rollins the third," she added, elaborating his title as she had done her own. "All right." I opened my eyes and took a look. She was a looker, too, even though you could tell she'd been crying. The tears seemed to have magnified her eyes; they were blue the color of the Côte d'Azur, and her nose, still red through the powder, was broad but upturned in a graceful way—perhaps she'd had it fixed; I couldn't tell. Her cheekbones were high and the skin over them was drawn with tension, but her complexion was the kind they advertised on TV as coming from bottles and tubes. Maybe that's where hers came from, too, but I doubted it. Her mouth was almost a straight line, except for a slightly pendulous lower lip that suggested the beginnings of a perennial pout. It was a striking face; it was a face under stress, devoid of any hint of intelligence or stupidity. It was a California face.

"When did he shoot himself?" I turned my light on, too.

"At six o'clock this evening. Look, I'm all right, now. You don't have to listen to all this."

"It's okay. How long had he been home?"

"Four months." Her eyes started to well up but she shook away the tears with determination. "Four months and two days."

"They've definitely said it was suicide?"

She gave me a funny look.

"What else? They heard the shot and found him in the den with the gun in his hand."

"It might have been an accident. People have been known to kill themselves while cleaning guns."

"He wasn't stupid."

"I didn't say—"

"Or careless. Look, he did it deliberately. That's all there is to it. He couldn't stand what they were going to put him through. I understand that. Boy, do I ever." The muscles in those high cheekbones twitched.

"Do you have any other brothers and sisters?"

"Nope. That was it. The last of the Rollins line." From the way she said it, I couldn't tell if it meant anything to her.

"Will your parents be there?"

"Haven't any of them, either. My mother died when I was fourteen. Cancer."

"And your father?" This was sounding grimmer all the time.

"Oh, he died in 1970. A coronary."

"So there's just you."

"Well, there is Yvonne. My stepmother." She volunteered it in a neutral tone.

"Are you close?"

She shrugged.

"Off and on." She looked away with a troubled expression. "Before I left home—when she first—when she married my father—we got on pretty well." She gave another of her imitation laughs, remembering. "She won us over." It sounded like it had been a battle.

"Well, I expect you'll pull together now."

"Yeah, I guess." She didn't sound convinced. She started to chew on a red thumbnail, then thought better of it and jerked her hand away with distaste. "Could I trouble you for a cigarette?"

"No trouble." I handed her the pack and she helped herself.

"I came away so fast I forgot everything. Thanks."

I shook out the match and decided to turn off our overhead lights. The renewed acquaintance with the darkness was settling for both of us, and we smoked for a time in silence. Leaning back in our chairs, lying next to each other and with my arm back around her shoulders, it was almost like being in bed together.

"Do you live in Washington?"

"I'm doing graduate work at Georgetown, yes."

"In what?"

10

"Anthropology." Our voices seemed quieter and more intimate in the dark. It really was like bed. "What do you do?"

This was always the strange part. For a moment I toyed with the idea of telling her I was an analyst and not to worry, I wasn't charging her anything for this session.

"I'm a detective."

For a moment she stiffened against my arm, then relaxed and twisted around to her side, facing me.

"Really? A detective?"

"Yes."

"Huh. I never met a detective in my life, I don't think." She lay on her back again and stared at the ceiling. "You see them on television all the time, of course. Are you a cop?"

"No. I'm a private investigator."

"That's good. Cops make me nervous. Like the military." Her voice turned hard and rose slightly.

"I've been a cop—and in the military."

She chose to ignore this.

"Let me ask you something. All those television programs—you know, like *Columbo?* Is it anything like that?"

"Sometimes. Not too much. Mainly it's less sensational—unless you count divorce cases and related items."

"A detective. That really blows my mind."

"Most of us brush our teeth just like everybody else."

She thrust herself up on one elbow and peered at me in an anxious posture.

"I didn't mean to be offensive. It's just that I—"

11

"Take it easy," I said, not moving. "I'm fine. And you've got a lot on your mind. Maybe you should try to get some sleep."

She sighed.

"I probably should."

We lay in silence. I pretended to doze off and she pretended to doze off.

When she thought I was out, she started to cry again, softly, carefully, and unhooked herself gingerly from my arm so as not to put it to sleep—which it was.

It wasn't yet dawn when we landed, and I had finally managed to get some shut-eye. So had Shelly Bettina Rollins, though she'd streaked her mascara again before succeeding. Lights in the overhead racks blinked on. There were the groans and sighs of stretching, and a fumbling on the floor for missing shoes and other vanished items.

I buttoned my shirt and slipped up my tie. Shelly examined herself in her compact mirror.

"Oh, my God. I'm a sight. Don't look," she instructed again. I assured her that I wouldn't and turned to stare out the window at LA International, swathed in early-morning fog from the coast, which might or might not burn off later in the day. You could never tell with June.

Shelly decided the major repairs were in order and, ignoring the stewardesses' request to remain seated until the plane had come to a complete stop, she squeezed past other unheeding passengers and made her way to the ladies'.

When she came back, the plane was almost empty and I was on my feet, getting down my hat and topcoat from the rack.

"Is this yours?" I offered her a snazzy leather driving

coat and she accepted with a little nod, letting me help her into it. She had a hat up there, too, as it turned out, a light woolen beret that stretched over her bun but clashed with her Pucci scarf.

"I told you I came away in a hurry." She took the beret and stuffed it into her coat pocket, then patted around the seat and ran fingers through the crevices between the cushions.

"Are you missing anything?"

"Just my mind. Fortunately, I've got plenty of clothes out here. All right."

I let her slip past me and followed her to the exit.

We had the long moving platform to the baggage claim pretty much to ourselves. There was a dreamlike quality to the scene. We had just covered three thousand miles and plunked ourselves down in a depopulated world of moving parts. It felt odd. Maybe airports always felt odd at 4:00 A.M.

Shelly Rollins felt it more than I did. She was tired and upset and disoriented, and she stared at the airport posters done by Los Angeles schoolchildren with unseeing eyes as the moving platform floated us past them.

"Is there anyone here to meet you?" I asked.

"Gee, I don't know. I don't think so. They didn't know how fast I could catch a plane. I certainly don't suppose they'd rise and shine to be down here at this hour."

Here was my cue, although she hadn't realized it.

"Where do you live? I'll run you home."

She blinked.

"Could you? In Brentwood. Do you have a car here?"

"No, but I'm planning on renting one. Brentwood's no trouble."

Brentwood wasn't any trouble. We found our bags waiting for us, revolving on the luggage carrousel like the two lonely horses they were. There was no traffic on the San Diego Freeway yet.

Shelly's family, or what was left of it, lived in a majestic white house with an elaborate circular drive leading up to and away from it. Westlake Avenue was prosperous-looking, with well-cultivated elm trees whose overhanging boughs made a year-round canopy for the road. The house appeared to be asleep when we pulled up, and our arrival didn't wake it.

"Have you got a key?"

"Yes." She fished it out. I took her suitcase from the back seat and set it down by the large green front door.

"Well, here you are, safe and sound." I looked down at her, but not far; she was pretty tall. "I'm sorry about your brother."

She shrugged and held out a hand.

"I'm all cried out at the moment. When I'm through being numb I'll probably start up again."

"You're among friends. They'll look after you now."

"Yes." She didn't seem too sure. "Look, I want to thank you for everything, Mr. Brill—"

"Mark."

She smiled sleepily.

"Mark. I don't know how I would have made it without you."

"You're a strong girl. You would have."

"Well—" She let go of my hand uncertainly and stared up at the windows of the house behind her, their white shades drawn like cataracts. "I'm so glad to have met a real detective."

"Here. Have a souvenir of the great moment." I pulled out my wallet and handed her a card.

She thanked me, put it in her pocket, and waited until I was halfway down the drive before starting to open the door to the house. Then she moved out of my rear-view mirror, swallowed up by the big white house.

2 I reached my two-room studio in Westwood by six, and slid into bed without setting the alarm. What would be would be, and I wasn't getting any younger.

I woke up, feeling decent, by noon, showered, shaved, and drove north on Sepulveda to my office, which was a one-flight walk-up in Westwood Village itself. I made a large pot of coffee and started going through a month's backlog of mail that was important enough to save but not worth forwarding: bills, political fund-raising circulars, white sales, and real estate offers concerning land that belonged to the Indians. There was a check I hadn't expected to see from a former client. I plowed through it all, then called my answering service and asked for details. That backlog wasn't very large—I kept in touch with them from Washington—or very interesting. By two I was finished with the whole thing and listening to the radio, with my feet propped comfortably up at the end of my secondhand Riviera sofa. Sometimes I've passed days in this posture, waiting for the folks to drop in with their bad news.

The radio news story was halfway over when I made the connection. Sergeant Harold Rollins III's death had been ruled an apparent suicide by the LA County Coroner's office. His stepmother was described as distraught, and in a recorded statement his fiancée said that Major Bruno's charges had upset him very much. I missed her name, but found that I was sitting up.

Shelly Rollins hadn't mentioned the fiancée—but then she was overwrought herself, and maybe she didn't even know. After all, she said they weren't all that close, and since he'd only been home four months, it was probably a recent development. It felt better to think that there was someone else, someone more her own age, to help Shelly Rollins share her grief.

They were interviewing Major Anthony J. Bruno now. In a flat, Midwestern monotone, he was making a statement: "This hasn't been very easy for me. . . . I try to tell myself I'm not . . . I felt I had a duty to the other men who were with me at the Swamp. . . . There's no need to tell you I wish this hadn't happened . . . any of it. . . ." The radio went on to announce that the Pentagon had determined that, as a result of this (and an allied incident involving members of another North Vietnamese prison camp), all charges involving collaboration with the enemy and the making of antiwar statements for counterpropaganda purposes were being dropped. In the specific case of Sergeant Rollins, the review board had already determined that there was insufficient evidence to support such charges, and had in fact attempted to dissuade Major Bruno from pressing them. Major Bruno had received his promotion from captain since returning Stateside.

There it was, a nice ironic news story, complete with

a statement from the grieving soon-to-have-been wife and a shattered reaction of military shock from the man it was easy to think of as Harold's murderer. I knew that was the way Shelly thought of him.

The news ended and an ad came on reminding me that I was hungry. I got up from the sofa, pulled out my tattered "Back in Five Minutes" placard, and hung it on the outside doorknob as I went downstairs. I cut through the supermarket parking lot and walked a block north on Broxton to a little Greek short-order place that doesn't do my stomach any good, where I had my idea of breakfast.

It was after three when I started back and the sun was finally beginning to burn through that fog. I trotted energetically up the stairs to my office, feeling better than I had in twenty-four hours. The heartburn would come later.

Nobody appeared to have seen my sign, which didn't faze me, either. I looked around at my outer office and decided I really had to get some newer magazines. Assuming somebody was going to be waiting out there, I doubted they would be interested in an October 2, 1972, edition of *Time* or the June 1973 *Harper's*. Maybe I should get material that didn't age so much, like *Playboy* or *National Geographic*.

I hadn't quite got comfortable on the couch when the outer door opened. Much to my surprise.

"Mr. Brill?" I knew that voice.

I got up and turned off the radio.

"Shelly?"

She was wearing a brown pants suit and a tentative smile. Both looked good on her.

18

"I hope you don't think I'm taking advantage of the card you gave me this morning to—"

"Here, sit down. That's what cards are for." She sat down carefully, stiffly, her head swiveling mechanically on her neck as she looked around.

"Like *Columbo?*"

"Kind of—I don't know." She seemed unsure of what was coming next. This made two of us. "You were more than five minutes," she observed. "I had to take a walk and come back." I apologized and asked if she'd like some coffee.

"Oh, yes, please. That would be very nice."

"It's freeze dried."

"That's all right."

We stopped this lively exchange while I put some water on the ring to boil and dished some Taster's Choice into my spare mug.

"Is this a business or a social call?" I asked, wanting to know.

"Business," she said quickly. "I guess." She must have seen my eyebrows go up. "I don't know. I'd like you to look into something for me. That's business, isn't it?"

"That's what it sounds like," I admitted. "What is it that wants checking out?" I hoped she wasn't going to say her brother's suicide, because the LA County Coroner's office was pretty reliable. Besides, if she told me now that she didn't think her brother was capable of killing himself, I wasn't prepared to take her word for it. They hadn't been that close.

"It's about my brother, and it's kind of hard to explain." She shifted awkwardly in her chair.

19

"Maybe I can help." I told her about the news account on the radio.

"That's just it," she said when I'd finished. "Now we'll never know."

"I'm not sure I follow you."

She gestured impatiently with her hand, leaning forward intensely.

"*Why* he did it. Because he was guilty of Major Bruno's charges, or because he couldn't take the harassment, the *possibility* of being convicted by a court-martial?"

I started pouring coffee.

"Do you think he was guilty?"

"That's not the point. With the Army refusing to look into it, my brother has gone to his grave with a stain on his name—the stain of an unproved accusation."

"Supposing it's proved. Wouldn't that be worse?"

"I'm not sure. No, I don't think so. Uncertainty is worse." She started to bite her thumbnail. "Besides, I don't believe he collaborated with the North Vietnamese. He didn't much care for the war, but that's not the same thing."

"No, it isn't. In other words, you want me to investigate Major Bruno's charges, interview other POWs who were there, that sort of thing?"

She nodded.

"If the Army won't take the trouble, I guess it's up to me."

I didn't feel like arguing about this point of view. I handed her her coffee and offered sugar and Preem, both of which she declined.

"You realize this could run into money," I said, sitting down again.

20

"Money?"

I looked at her. She hadn't realized it.

"Yes, I generally get a hundred dollars a day plus expenses."

She sat back with a sigh of relief.

"Oh, that's all right. I have that kind of money."

"You're sure?"

"Certainly I'm sure. I don't like your tone." She frosted over very fast.

"Well, don't get me wrong. It's just that you said you were in graduate school and a hundred a day plus is going to mount up after a few days."

"All right, all right. Never mind about all that. I've got money of my own. I wasn't flying on that plane last night to save the 20-per-cent air fare."

Touché. I thought of her home in Brentwood and mentally agreed she was right. The subject of money upset her; however democratic and breakaway she was in other respects, when it came to buying she didn't like to haggle.

"Well, will you take on the assignment?"

"Let me ask you some questions first. They may not always seem like relevant questions but you'll have to let me go about this in my own way, okay?"

"Okay." She thawed. "And I'm sorry if I was testy. I didn't get much sleep last night—as you know—and I've been trying to keep Yvonne together and fend off reporters ever since you took me home this morning."

She smiled and showed me the lines of fatigue her make-up was supposed to conceal around her eyes and mouth. I rummaged around in my desk and found a pencil with a new point, opened my notebook, and rapidly jotted down some background information while she sat and waited.

"All right, Shelly, how—"

"No one calls me that," she interrupted, eager to be helpful and friendly.

"What do they call you?"

"Bunny. It's been my nickname since sixth grade. Don't ask me why."

"I won't." Bunny, I saw at once, fitted her much better. "How old are you, Bunny?"

Her eyes widened.

"Is that important?"

"For the record, yes. If I know it for certain I don't have to worry about your legal right to employ my services—against the wishes of, say, your guardian."

"I'm twenty-four."

"How old was Harold?"

"Twenty-five." She bit her lip. "No one called him Harold, either." I looked up. "His nickname was Rollo."

"Very useful. It could be derived from either Harold or Rollins, couldn't it?"

"That was the idea, I guess."

"Tell me about Rollo."

She sighed.

"God, how can you sum up someone you've known almost all your life?" She frowned in concentration, trying to figure out where to begin.

"Were you ever close?" I asked, trying to be helpful.

"When we were kids. Moving around from base to base, we were the only social constants in each other's lives, and—"

"From base to base?"

22

"We were army brats. Where Dad went, we went; Texas, Cape Cod, Oklahoma—"

"Your father was an army man?" I put down my pencil.

"I thought you knew. I don't know why," she added, to no one in particular. "Brigadier General Harold Rollins. If you were in Korea you must have heard of him."

"I wasn't and I didn't," I confessed. This seemed to confuse her, but I sensed the effect was not entirely negative.

"You and Rollo were close on the army bases?" I prompted.

"I guess we were close until Mom died. Then Rollo started acting stranger and stranger."

"Did he have a breakdown?"

"Not exactly," she answered, drawling. "But he was recommended for psychiatric treatment by the guidance counselor at the base school in Tulsa."

"Did he get it?"

She shook her head.

"Dad didn't believe in anything like that. He just thought Rollo ought to shape up, as he put it. He was very big on shaping up. I suppose Rollo and I took after our mother more than him and he just never did understand either of us. It was all right for me to be sensitive, quote unquote, but Rollo was just a sissy."

"Was he? A sissy?" I added when she did not seem to understand my question.

"I don't think so, no. He liked girls and he went out with them and all. He just would rather have been a painter than—" She finished the sentence with an amorphous gesture of her hands to indicate what Rollo had become.

"Your father retired eventually?"

"Finally, from active service. He took a post at Los Angeles Civic University in charge of their ROTC program. If only Mother could have lived to see it."

"How do you mean?"

"Well, as I understand it—and I got most of this from Rollo—Mother met and married Father during the war. She assumed, and I guess he let her assume, that this wasn't a career thing and that when it was over, he'd get out. But he didn't." She looked up across the desk at me. "I don't think she ever was reconciled to that. She wasn't suited to be an army wife. She had an artistic temperament." She tested the phrase and eyed me again for approval.

"Go on."

"Well, then she got sick and died—it was all very fast, six months, in fact—and then it didn't matter any more. A year later Dad was out and handling ROTC, which she might have seen as a compromise—certainly we've lived in one place ever since."

"And then he remarried."

She sighed again.

"That's right. I suppose Yvonne was a much better wife from his point of view. She thrived on uniforms. She fancied herself as the General's lady, sitting next to him during all those cadet reviews and such."

"How'd Rollo take it?"

"Hard at first. We both did. No stepmother ever won a prize for popularity, I guess. But we got used to it. Yvonne's not bad when you get used to her airs and graces. And I'd have to say she took good care of us—and I mean *care*."

"Did you go to the same high school?"

"Brentwood High. I was the good student and Rollo was the cutup. I tried tutoring him in math one summer," she remembered.

"Cutup? As in hoodlum?"

"No, no, nothing like that. He just couldn't get his act together, you know? He was smart as a whip but he couldn't be bothered studying. He'd cram like crazy the night before finals and get by with C's and B minuses. He just couldn't be bothered."

"And still no psychiatrist or guidance counseling?"

She shook her head again.

"Yvonne tried to bring Dad round but there were some subjects he just wouldn't listen to reason on. Psychiatry was part of the Jewish conspiracy."

I digested this.

"Did Rollo have many friends at school?"

"Nobody close, if that's what you mean. Kids thought he was a scream—Rollo could be very funny—but he didn't really let people get close. Even me. Dad tried to push him into a friendship with Tony Bruno, but that only made it worse because Rollo realized he was just being held up as a kind of example for him—"

"Hold it, hold it. Back up. Tony Bruno? This wouldn't be Major Bruno?"

Her mouth dropped open in blank surprise.

"I'm sorry. God, it's really hard to tell all this. I keep leaving things out on the assumption that somehow everyone knows them. Common knowledge, so to speak."

"That's all right, just so we find out. Tony Bruno was in your father's ROTC program?"

She nodded.

"His great prize. Brilliant officer material and all that. Absolutely worshiped Dad, which was another

25

plus. He was five years older than Rollo and I guess he was everything Dad wanted his son to be. He was always over at the house."

"And Rollo didn't like him?"

"Hated his guts. Actually, I did, too. He was a pompous asshole," she said without a blush, "and the way he sucked up to Dad was shameful." She picked a piece of lint off her pant leg. "I guess I was right about him all along."

It was getting pretty incestuous.

"How did Lieutenant Bruno relate to Rollo?"

"Oh, he made a show of being big brother when Dad was around, clapping Rollo on the back and giving him all that shape-up jazz that he knew Dad loved to hear. I don't think there was any love lost either way, though."

"How'd Rollo wind up in the Army?"

"I'm not really sure. I was doing time at Bennington when it happened, so I don't know what all went on. Rollo started at LA Civic but he dropped out after a semester, and from the letters Yvonne sent me he seemed to be spending all his time at the beach. Of course that was when the big build-up in Vietnam was going on and they were drafting everybody with two legs. I recall writing to Rollo and asking him what he planned to do about it." She looked down at the floor. "He never answered my letter. Next thing I knew, he was enlisting. And, of course, Dad pulled a few strings and got him in with Tony. The theory being that he'd look out for Rollo. Ho, ho, ho," she concluded hollowly.

"Did you know what Rollo's views on the war were?"

"I said he wasn't stupid," she flashed, color rising to her cheeks. "I was home Christmas of—" She paused and did a little mental arithmetic. "Nineteen sixty-eight, it must have been, and we had one of our rare heart-to-heart talks."

"About the war?"

"About everything. The war was just part of it. Rollo was in the Army by then, stationed at Conway—outside Redondo Beach?"

I nodded.

"He treated it like a joke, talked about what he called the patent absurdity of attempting to attain a military victory in a situation where it just wasn't possible. He pointed out that if you won you lost, because the moment the VC surrendered—even assuming they could be brought to their knees after the French had failed to do it—what would happen then? The U.S. would pull out and they'd swarm right down through the Central Highlands again."

"How did he reconcile this with his being in the Army? Did he take the position of his country right or wrong?"

"It was all a kind of joke, I'm telling you. He didn't seem to care. When I asked him why he'd gone in, he said he heard the grass was greener in Saigon. Grass, get it?"

"I get it."

"I guess he felt he'd run out of options and was just too tired to fight him any more. This was a kind of lip-service escape for Rollo."

" 'Him' being your father."

"That's right."

"Did you hear from him in the service?"

"A couple of letters. He was at Pleiku. He drew some pictures of Vietnamese children and sent them to me." She was starting to sniffle.

"Did he comment on the war pro or con in his letters?"

"Not really. Of course it wouldn't have been very politic. I remember one letter of his saying 'We're here because we're here because we're here.' Another time he said he thought he was really getting his head together."

"Any references to Tony Bruno?"

"He called him 'that clown' a couple of times but never elaborated." She took out a freshly laundered handkerchief and dabbed at her eyes.

"Take it easy."

"I'm trying," she snapped. I felt I was running out of time. In a few more minutes she was going under and we'd have to continue this in a day or so.

"When was he captured?"

"August 17, 1969. They were ambushed on patrol. They were all killed except Tony and Rollo."

I wrote down the date.

"Did he mention any friends he'd made, either in prison or at Pleiku?"

"There were a couple of fellows he apparently got on with. A doctor named Fairland or Fairfield—that was it, Jake Fairfield, a navy doctor he met at the Swamp. Then there was another sergeant he talked about in one of his letters. Lewis Browne."

"With an *e w* or an *o u?*"

"I'd have to check the letter—*e w*, I think. They bunked together. Browne was a Negro and had to take a lot of flak about it, Rollo said."

That sounded like the Army I remembered.

"Do you have the letters? Can I see them?"

"They're at home. Do you have to?"

"They might give me some hints. This is pretty sparse and what you're asking for is a tall order."

"I know." She put away the handkerchief. "But he couldn't very well have been a raving antiwar activist out there if he made sergeant, could he?"

"Maybe not, but that doesn't solve our problem. Major Bruno's charges refer to his conduct while a prisoner of war. Prison camp can do funny things to men," I added, remembering a few horror stories of my own.

"Not that funny." Her mouth compressed in a straight line.

"Well, we'll see. Now let me just ask a couple more questions and we'll call it a day. Tell me about Rollo's fiancée. Did you know anything about that?"

"In a way I did and in a way I didn't. Her name's Margot Koontz"—she spelled it for me—"and she's a dental technician out in Woodland Hills. She was a member of the group that wore the POW bracelets, you know? And when Rollo landed at Clarke, she had a letter and a package waiting for him. His name was on the bracelet she wore. Anyway, Rollo wrote and thanked her, and when he got home they started dating. The rest is history."

Her ironic emphasis was beginning to grate on my nerves but I really couldn't blame her. She had no other way to let off steam.

"How's she taking this?"

"About how you'd expect. She's less than thrilled."

It was time to wrap up the conversation.

"You saw Rollo when he got home. How was he?"

"You mean physically? He was fifteen pounds lighter than I'd ever seen him."

"Mentally?"

"Together. He'd finally got his act together. Those were his very words, as a matter of fact. And I believed him." Her opinion was a challenge.

"One more question and we'll stop. Did he leave a suicide note?"

She blanched as though I'd struck her. Her mouth opened and closed but no words came out.

"I'm sorry, but did he? The news broadcast I heard didn't make any mention of it."

"No—not to my knowledge," she choked out.

"All right." I stood up and came around my desk. "You've given me some stuff to start on. Is the funeral set?"

"For tomorrow." She'd recovered her poise and rose to her feet, following me to the door. "Would you like to attend? The services are at eleven at Brentwood Episcopal. He'll be buried at Brentwood Rest—with full military honors, of course. The Army never forgets to lock its stable doors."

"Simmer down. I may show up. And I'll definitely stay in touch."

"At a hundred bucks a throw that's the least you can do." She regretted saying it as soon as she finished and gave me a lopsided smile to take the sting away. I decided to let her get away with it. She leaned up against the doorframe and wrote out a five-hundred-dollar check to make sure I'd stay in touch. We hadn't actually discussed it, but it looked like I was taking her case.

3 I spent the rest of the afternoon filling in the background of the case. I called Pete Ericson, a detective I knew in Saint Louis whose back I'd scratched a couple of times, and asked him to get in touch with the people at the Army Record Center there and find out whether Sgt. Lewis Browne, who'd been stationed at Pleiku or thereabouts in the first part of 1969, was still alive and kicking, and if so, where. Also I wanted him to try to locate a navy doctor named Fairfield, first name Jake or possibly Jacob, who'd been in a North Vietnamese POW camp nicknamed "the Swamp" in the latter part of '69. Pete said he'd check it out and get back to me.

Then I drove downtown to have a look at some back issues of the LA *Times* and at the coroner's report, just for the hell of it. According to the deposition of Sergeant Rollins' stepmother, Rollins had been despondent upon learning of Major Bruno's charges. He had talked with her in the den of their Brentwood home shortly before dinner. Mrs. Rollins had left him alone in the room and gone to talk to the cook, when the two women heard a single shot. Returning to the den, they found Rollins prone and motionless beside what had been General Rollins' desk. In his hand was a .45-caliber service revolver that had belonged to the General and which Mrs. Rollins kept loaded in the desk drawer in case of prowlers. One shot had been fired from the weapon at point-blank range into the deceased's right temple. Death had been instantaneous. And messy. According to the report, blood and brain matter had spattered about a good deal and some had landed on the revolver's custom-made ivory handles. (The General, it seems, had been an admirer of General Patton.) There was no trace of a suicide note.

Mrs. Rollins' account was borne out by the cook, whose name captured my attention briefly: Clarisse Marengo, who gave her birthplace as Martinique. Both women were described as "distraught," and Rollins' fiancée, who was also interviewed, with a view to ascertaining Rollins' state of mind (although she hadn't seen him since four that afternoon), was described as "incoherent."

The only fingerprints on the gun were those of the deceased, and they were captured quite vividly with the aid of his own blood. He had apparently squeezed the handle of the weapon convulsively in his death spasms.

When I got home, I poured myself a drink, threw together a decent dinner, and checked with my service. Pete Ericson hadn't left word. I'd talked to him about four, which meant it had been six in Saint Louis. The Record Center was closed there and I was going to have to wait until midmorning sometime for results.

Which left me plenty of time to attend Harold Rollins' funeral.

There are people in this world who enjoy a good funeral. They are the same kinds of professional observers who crowd the open-access seats in our courtrooms and make a life style out of other people's tragedies. In less overt form, they can be found yelling instructions from the bleachers and Monday-morning quarterbacking a Rams game. As fans, they don't bother me so much; at least they are committed to opinions, however silly. As professional mourners and silent celebrators of grief, they horrify me. Their interest in the fate of people with whom they have no legitimate concern or compassion appears to me simply ghoulish.

All of which is a fancy lead-in to the fact that Brentwood Episcopal the next morning at eleven was crammed with them. Sergeant Rollins' suicide was something everyone could enjoy. It had all the classic elements of ghoul-inspiring fascination: the death itself, with the poor man's brains blown to kingdom come, the story behind the death, with its lurid and disgraceful implications, the presence of the press, those impartial Eumenides with their color-television cameras; yes, a regular field day. And the military helped out by launching Sergeant Rollins' escape from this world with all the ritual and precision of a NASA send-off. They'd all deny it if you confronted them, of course. Ritual was a way of channeling grief and honoring the passing of an honorable man. Everyone packed into Brentwood Episcopal that morning had nothing better to do than listen to the minister equivocate on the subject of Harold Rollins and the meaning of his life.

Afterward, the limousines lumbered off for the cemetery and I climbed into my old Ford and followed them, eager for a glimpse of the immediate family. So far, all I could make out of Bunny Rollins and her stepmother were two distant figures in black. The older woman wore an impenetrable veil.

At the cemetery the falderal continued, with the honor guard firing blanks into the air and the coffin being slid out from underneath the American flag, which was then folded in the prescribed manner and presented to Mrs. Rollins as a souvenir of the occasion. Then it began to fall apart, with a lieutenant colonel offering Mrs. Rollins his arm as he escorted her back to the Cadillac, and the rest of the people, including the television cameras, breaking camp. I was so busy looking around for Bunny that I didn't notice her come up behind me. She looked indecently good in black.

"Having a good time?"

"So-so. I didn't see anyone who looked like Margot Koontz."

"That's because she isn't here. She was too shook up. I hardly blame her. And I don't think Yvonne was too encouraging, either."

"Oh, no?"

She smiled weakly.

"Dental technicians are a little thin for her blood."

"I see. Listen, did you find your brother's letters?"

"I'll have them for you this evening," she promised. "You're supposed to come by anyway."

"Oh?"

"Yvonne wants to have a word with you."

"You told her about hiring me?"

"Why not? It's perfectly legal, isn't it? Somebody's got to do something." She was growing indignant and

34

forgetting the car that was waiting to take her back to the parade.

"It's perfectly legal."

"What's the matter? Don't tell me she can buy you off."

"She can't, but I can walk off. And I will, too, if you don't stop treating me like one of the court musicians. What time should I stop by?" I went on, before she had time to make a scene.

"Around eight."

"I'll see you then," I said, and headed for my car.

When I looked back, she was still standing there, one black-gloved hand resting on top of a thick alabaster gravestone, staring unhappily at the ground. As I watched, another uniformed gent came to get her and she went quietly.

Back at my office, I had a message from Pete Ericson and I returned his call. He told me that I would find Lewis Browne, with an *e*, in Roxbury, Massachusetts, a suburb of Boston, at 1365 Pringle Avenue. Browne had been wounded in action, and was receiving special veterans' benefits. Dr. Jacob Fairfield was to be found at 315 West Seventy-eighth Street, and was currently attached to Mount Sinai Hospital in New York, as a surgeon.

"Look, Pete, do me one more favor, will you?"

"Anything you say, buddy boy. I'll take it out in trade when I need odd jobs done in LA."

"Fair enough. I want you to make a list with names and addresses of all the military personnel who were in a prisoner-of-war camp known as the Swamp."

"Jesus, Mark—"

"I know it's a lot. Look, I'll narrow it down. Let's just make it from August 20, 1969, on. Is that better?"

"Well, some," he grumbled. "The Swamp?"

"That's right. And Pete, take your time. I don't know if I'm even going to need it."

"All righty, Mark boy. This is your show."

I thanked him, hung up, and looked at my watch. It wasn't yet three-thirty and I decided to see if I could talk to Margot Koontz. I'd copied her Woodland Hills address down from the coroner's report and I started out for the valley. If she hadn't been able to make it to the funeral she probably wasn't at work, either, so I dismissed the idea of trying her office and drove to her home. It turned out to be one of those huge singles apartment complexes built like blockhouses around a series of swimming pools and other recreational facilities, designed for fun-loving swinging types who were unencumbered by children, spouses, or pets.

I got lost several times trying to locate the correct blockhouse, found it at last, and took an elevator to the second floor. Then I had to walk down an endless gloomy corridor before arriving at the right door. I knew it was the right door because someone had pasted one of those punch-letter tapes below the peephole. It was labeled simply "Koontz." I rang the buzzer and waited for a few moments. I thought I heard voices coming from inside, and then footsteps.

"Who is it?"

"My name is Brill," I said to someone I couldn't see. "Bunny Rollins sent me." It wasn't really the truth, but in a way it was.

"Are you with the press?" the voice demanded.

"No."

There was another moment's hesitation and another murmured exchange before the door was opened by a short woman who looked about thirty. Her brown hair was cut in a pageboy and she wore thick-lensed, unattractive glasses.

"I'm here to talk to Margot Koontz," I said. "Are you—"

"I'm her sister," she replied, motioning me in. "Just a minute and I'll get her." She pointed to some cheap furniture that was scattered aimlessly about and disappeared. I took up residence in an armchair that looked better than it felt. The apartment was spotlessly clean, and a large window on the other side of a fold-out dining table looked down on the pool. I was wrong about the absence of children. There were several, splashing about and making noise, which the window rendered faint, while their mothers and baby-sitters tried to soak up some of the unwilling June sun.

"Mr. Brill?" I turned and saw a younger, more attractive version of the sister. Margot Koontz was a little taller, a little thinner, and a little blonder. And she didn't wear glasses. At the moment she wasn't wearing any make-up and her eyes were bleary, puffy, and red. I got up and explained who I was.

"I don't understand." She waved me back to my seat and sat down on the convertible sofa across from me. "Didn't the police go through all of this? They certainly asked me a lot of questions." Her hands played restlessly in her lap as she spoke.

"I'm not investigating the suicide. Sergeant Rollins' sister hired me to find out what I could about the truth or falsehood of Major Bruno's charges."

"They're false," she answered promptly, but without energy.

"Do you have any proof?"

"How can I? I wasn't there with him, was I?" One of the restless hands clawed absently through her hair. "It just isn't true, that's all. He would have told me. He told me about the torturing and all."

"He was tortured at the Swamp?"

"Was he ever. His entire back was covered with—" She stopped, self-consciously.

"Please go on."

"I—" She groped for what she wanted to say. "I'd rather not."

"I wish you would. I know it must be very painful and perhaps even embarrassing for you to have me here asking these questions, but it would be very important for all of us if we could find out the truth."

"I know the truth," she repeated stubbornly. "And nothing anyone at the Pentagon says or doesn't say is going to change my mind."

As she spoke, my eyes traveled around the room and came to rest on a set of suitcases sitting beside the front door. I'd seen them before but somehow they hadn't clicked. I had assumed that they belonged to Margot Koontz's elder sister, who'd come to stay with her. Now I knew better. There was an olive-drab duffel bag with black lettering stenciled on it stuffed into the corner, and a green combat jacket was lying across the top of a man's Val Pack. Harold Rollins had been living here for some period of time, and recently; and now his suitcases were packed and ready, all dressed up with no place to go because their owner had already passed the customs barrier where all luggage is sent back.

Margot Koontz caught me looking at the bags and stopped in midsentence. I turned and faced her.

"Miss Koontz, I've come here prepared to believe you. I want to believe you. My client wants to believe you. Do you know her?"

She nodded slightly.

"Yeah, she's all right."

"I think so, too. Now I'm not asking you to invent a story, but if you can think of *anything*, anything at all that might help, I wish you'd tell me about it, or give me the go-ahead to keep asking you what questions I can come up with."

"It won't bring him back," she said tonelessly.

"It might bring back his honor."

The sister emerged from the bedroom wearing a bathrobe and pool clogs, with a towel thrown over her shoulder.

"Is everything all right?" she asked, without really directing her question to either of us.

"I'm fine, Jan. Jan, have you met Mr. Brill?" I stood up.

"How do you do?"

"Yeah, we've met," Jan responded indifferently. "If it's all right I'm goin' down to the pool."

"Sure. You go on ahead."

"You want a Coke from the machine?"

"That's all right." She turned to me. "Maybe you would, Mr. Brill?"

"Maybe I could trouble you for a cup of instant coffee." I wanted to give her something to do with her hands.

"Sure. I'm sorry. I guess I'm—"

"That's all right, really."

"Well, I'm on my way," the older sister interrupted.

"Have a nice time." We stood still and watched her leave. "Let's go into the kitchen, why don't we," she suggested when the door had closed.

"Fine with me."

"You mustn't mind Jan," she said, leading the way. "She's very shy and she means well. It's only that this thing has really confused her and she doesn't know how to react to all of it—the part about Rollo's living here and all. We're not that close. The whole thing's been a terrible shock for her."

"You seem to be bearing up pretty well under the strain."

"Yeah, right. If you were on as many tranquilizers as I am right now, your nerve ends would all be dead, too."

"I see."

"One of the advantages of being a dental technician. God knows I haven't abused it until now. It's funny. It hasn't robbed me of any of my feelings, it just kind of saps your energy to express them, at least that's how it feels to me. I mean, I was hysterical for two days straight, beginning Wednesday night?" She looked at me, ending the statement on an upturned interrogative. I nodded.

"And now, I just can't muster up the energy to be hysterical. It's weird." She opened cupboards and began mechanically pulling down cups and saucers and heating up water. "Are you sure you don't mind instant? I can make real."

"Instant is fine. I won't be staying all that long."

She almost shrugged and continued with her preparations.

"How long had Rollo been living here?"

"Almost two months."

"Did he talk in his sleep?"

She whirled around as though I'd yanked her by an invisible string, knocking a coffee cup to the floor, where it shattered.

"Who told you that? Where did you hear that?"

"Take it easy." I bent down to pick up the pieces of cup.

"I want to know where you found that out," she insisted, her voice becoming shrill.

"I didn't find it out, I just asked you," I assured her. "Lots of veterans have nightmares, particularly those who've been under combat strain or spent time in POW camps."

"Oh." She seemed uncertain, and a little reluctant to accept my answer. She thought Rollo's having nightmares was unique.

Opening the door underneath the sink, I found the garbage bag, and put in the chips of the coffee cup; there were too many of them to glue it back together again.

"I'm sorry about the cup."

"What? Oh, that's all right. It's nice to know those tranqs aren't all that good." She turned and pulled down another cup, carefully filled it with boiling water, and stirred in the coffee. "How do you take yours?"

"Black is fine."

I followed her back to the dining area, carrying our coffee, and sat down opposite her. The sun was beginning to stream in through the window between us as though it were carving a route through the fog, which just happened to take it in our direction.

"Rollo had nightmares," I prompted, and she nodded without commenting. "Every night?"

"Not that often. Not the real bad ones. They were once or twice a week."

"What were they like?"

She set down her coffee cup and stared out the window, absorbed in the children who were running amuck down there. I wondered if she was associating any of them with burnt-out hopes of her own.

"He used to wake up screaming," she said, not taking her eyes off the window. "I mean literally screaming—and bathed in sweat."

"Screaming words or just screaming?"

"Words at first, and then just screaming until he woke himself up. It would begin softly, with him muttering something. Sometimes I was awake for that part and other times I didn't come in until later. After a while, the mumbling would get more distinct, you know?" Still she couldn't face me. "It sounded like he was saying 'No more, no more,' and sometimes it was 'No more killing, no more killing,' repeated many times and getting louder and louder all the time, until he'd wake up screaming 'No more killing!' at the top of his lungs. The neighbors complained," she threw in.

"No more killing? Did you understand him to be talking about the war in general?"

"I don't know what he was talking about. I tried mentioning it to him once or twice after they were over, but he always refused to discuss it."

"What happened when he heard about Major Bruno's charges? How did he act? Did he seem frightened, or upset?"

"We heard about it on the six o'clock news, Tuesday."

42

She took a cigarette out of a box on the table and I lit it for her. "It was strange; like I tried to tell the police, he didn't seem frightened at all. I was," she remembered.

"How did he seem?"

"Excited, very het up." She searched for words, casting her eyes to the ceiling. "Elated?"

"He seemed elated?"

"Overjoyed. He said something about 'If that's the way they want to play, that's fine with me.' "

"He said that, and you told the police?"

"Well, no, I didn't actually tell them that part. See, I was hysterical at the time, like I said, and I wasn't making too much sense. Oh, and that night—Tuesday—he had the dream again, the one about stop the killing."

I didn't want to take notes in front of her but the temptation was almost irresistible.

"One last question, Miss Koontz, and then I'll be on my way."

"No hurry."

She didn't seem to be in one.

"Rollo was living here?"

She nodded heavily, almost as though she were falling asleep, coffee or no coffee. Those tranqs packed a wallop.

"What made him go home Wednesday night?"

"What?"

"Why was he at home Wednesday when the—uh—when it happened?"

"Search me. I mean I don't know why he did it there. Unless it was to spare me or something. His mother asked him over."

"Mrs. Rollins?"

"She said she wanted to talk to him about the charges.

He didn't want to go, I don't think, but I got the impression she was very insistent about it."

I got up.

"You don't like her much, do you?"

She looked up at me slowly, her eyes wide with fatigued innocence.

"Me? What's she got to do with me?"

She had a point. She didn't have anything to do with her. Any more.

4 The Rollins home loomed larger in the evening than it had during the early hours of the morning when I had first seen it. The last rays of the summer sun, persisting until after eight, bounced off the house's windows as though the panes were bulletproof.

An impassive butler who had known better days but not a better job opened the door and murmured that I was expected. His tone of decorous neutrality carefully implied that I might have been king or peasant, it was all the same to him. So long as I was expected.

He led me through the Spanish-tiled foyer, which was dark and cool, and into the den, which was really more like a library. From the descriptions, I had expected to find the place crammed with war mementos of an Old Campaigner—something I wasn't sure I was up to—but the room, though obviously belonging to someone with a military bent, had been furnished with tasteful restraint. It was paneled in dark wood, probably oak, with a low, intimate ceiling and polished wide-plank floor. The wainscoting was very convincing eighteenth century. There was a brighter rectangular patch on the floor, which showed me that a rug had recently been removed from in front of a large mahogany desk. Probably it matched the colorful Indian one by the French windows, which opened onto what looked like a large garden, a pool, and a white wrought-iron summerhouse. The rug was probably being cleaned and would no doubt shortly find its way back into this charming room.

There was small doubt in my mind that the den, and the house itself, reflected Mrs. Rollins' taste and restraint. Perhaps it was the choice of furniture, or the quiet arrangement of the General's war photographs on one wall juxtaposed with some handsomely framed Audubon prints above his desk. The absence of medals and trophies—though there were one or two—tended to suggest a becoming modesty, while a carved wooden pipe rack, complete with pipes of differing character, and a comfortable-looking sofa blended in an assured, masculine presence. Over a small fieldstone fireplace hung an eighteenth-century flintlock.

The weird thing, of course, was that the man whose room this was supposed to be had been dead for three years. I caught myself wondering how many little touches—like those Quimper vases on either end of the mantel—had been added after the General had been in no position to object. No, not object, for he could hardly have begrudged the decorator whose impeccable taste had created this hideaway; but he certainly would no longer profit by additional refinements.

Strictly speaking though, this wasn't fair, either. After all, the room could and should be used for purposes other than as a museum. In addition to the rows of Moroccan red-leather-bound military volumes, someone had placed a television set discreetly in one corner, and the pool table across from the desk looked as though it had been used recently.

Next to the pool table was a bar that had also seen recent use, as two Old Fashioned glasses with their swizzle sticks still in them proclaimed.

No one had yet been moved to join me, and I didn't feel cheeky enough to make myself a drink.

Two days ago a young man had shot himself here, though nothing except the absent rug indicated anything amiss. I found myself circling the room and trying to reconstruct the scene in my mind. Those French doors, for instance: Were they open or closed? Closed, according to the coroner's report. And the gun? That was in the desk, of course.

I pulled open the desk drawer and found myself staring at the ivory-handled revolver. Mrs. Rollins was still on guard for prowlers. I picked it up and examined the chambers. They were full. He must have opened the drawer, pulled out the gun, and stood here in the middle of this patch of absent rug . . .

I stopped. Overhead I could hear a crash and the sounds of voices raised in angry debate. Women's voices. Mrs. Rollins' and her stepdaughter's no doubt. I wondered if they were tossing Quimper vases at each other and why. Probably over me. I should have felt flattered.

I put the revolver back into the desk drawer and closed it. Then I stood in the center of the bare patch of floor nearest the desk and slowly turned three hundred and sixty degrees, trying to see where the bullet had wound up. I couldn't remember offhand what the ballistics boys had said. I studied the walls and the ceiling from my eye level up, assuming that Rollins had angled the barrel upward when he had fired—the case with most temple-shooting suicides—but I couldn't find any trace. I gave it up; it wasn't what I was here for, anyway. Just occupational curiosity.

On the desk were several photographs. One looked like a honeymoon shot of General Rollins and his wife. I picked it up and studied it. The man in the picture was tall and spare and straight, with a crinkled squinting smile of masculine assuredness and maturity. His hair was streaked with gray and slightly curly. He was in uniform with his hat tucked correctly under one arm. His other arm was over the shoulders of a woman much shorter and much younger than himself. She had long wavy dark hair and was looking up at him with an adoring smile, revealing a wide mouth filled with good-looking teeth. She wore a dark two-piece bathing suit— they seemed to be standing in front of some sort of tropical bungalow, but the background was fuzzy—and she possessed a provocative figure. Her legs were particularly good. It was a funny picture; he looked ready for parade drill and she was about to enter a beauty contest.

What chiefly interested me about the picture was that it had been airbrushed in a professional manner, though the shot itself was obviously an amateur candid and the subjects had posed for it self-consciously. For a vacation or honeymoon picture, reality hadn't been good enough.

There were three more photos on the desk, one of a younger version of the General, in the uniform of a private, second class. Harold Rollins III was smiling easily into the camera, leaning against a tree in a garden —perhaps the one behind the house. His smile was both infectious and self-mocking. It seemed to be saying how surprised its owner was to find himself where he was, how amiably confused by it all, and that he was not quite certain how seriously to take the moment when the picture was snapped. There was a baby picture of Bunny sitting in a party dress on a floor somewhere, her hair full of ribbons and curls and a pair of white frilly panties peeping out at the camera in childish indifference. Her face had since fulfilled all its cherubic promise.

The last photo was a brown-and-white formal portrait of a young man in the uniform of a second lieutenant. His jaw was set as though he were clenching it, and his eyes deliberately ignored the camera as they stared out into the future. The eyes were clear, the mouth firm, and the lips compressed into a hard line of manly determination. Lieutenant Bruno, of course. He looked as though he were posing for a recruiting poster. Maybe he thought he was.

As I set down this last photograph, the door behind me opened and Bunny stepped in, closed the door, and leaned against it. Her skin was whiter than I'd known it and she clutched a packet nervously in her hands. A strand of blonde hair had escaped the clutch of her bun and trailed over her forehead.

"She's coming," she said, breathing in the wrong places.

"Your stepmother?"

She nodded vigorously.

"And I'm afraid she's had a few. It's been a trying day," she added defensively, in response to my look. "She's got a right to be upset."

"I didn't realize she and Rollo were that close. Are those his letters?"

"They're all here. You'll take good care of them, won't you?"

I told her I would and asked if she had any photographs of Rollo she could let me have, since I might have to show his picture to fellow prisoners who never knew him by name.

"I thought of that. You'll find some snapshots in there." She went over to the bar. "Did you see the one on the desk? Well, there's that one and some others taken at Pleiku. Anything earlier wouldn't be any help, would it?"

"Probably not. I'll check them out and let you know if I need any more, and I'll make copies of these if I have to use them. Are you having a drink?"

"Yes. Oh, for heaven's sake, I'm so sorry. Here I am, standing right here and I didn't even ask if you'd like to join me. Would you?"

"I think perhaps Mr. Brill would, Bunny. That was probably the point behind his question. Am I right, Mr. Brill?"

She had opened the door so gently (and kept it so well oiled) that neither of us had heard Mrs. Rollins enter.

She wasn't what I'd expected. Or, rather, she was, but I hadn't expected to find it so wonderfully preserved. By rights, Yvonne Rollins couldn't have been much less than forty-five but she looked a full ten years younger. She had kept her figure intact, and although she was wearing a tailored beige cotton summer suit, its lines failed to conceal a voluptuous bosom, which had been hidden from view in the photograph on the desk. Her hair was a shiny russet with no trace of gray, though I suspected Clairol had a hand in that, and her eyes were bright and green and reminded me of a cat's. She wasn't as tall as Bunny, or as steady on her feet; as I'd been told, she'd had a few. She was swaying, ever so slightly, as she stood there, taking me apart and putting me back together with those provocative eyes, and when she spoke, her voice lilted with the faint traces of a Southern accent.

"Would you care for something?" she asked.

"I'll take an Old Fashioned, if that's what's in vogue," I offered.

"Yes, that's what's in vogue, I think. Bunny dear, now that you have yours, would you mind making one for Mr. Brill and me? And then, if you'll oblige me, I'd like to talk to Mr. Brill alone." Bunny said nothing but started in on the drinks. "Please sit down, Mr. Brill." She waved me airily to the couch. "I do apologize for having kept you waiting so long."

"That's quite all right. This is a lovely room."

"Yes, isn't it?" She seemed startled by my observation and looked around quickly, surveying her handiwork. "Of course I have a different reaction to it at the moment."

"I'm sorry about your stepson's death."

"Of course you are," she said, and there let matters hang. Clearly, she had no intention of continuing the conversation until Bunny had left the room, so we waited awkwardly for her to deliver our drinks and follow through with the game plan.

"Thank you, my dear," she said when Bunny dropped them off. "Now run along, won't you, and let me have some conference with Mr. Brill."

"I'm not a child, Yvonne." She cast an anxious glance in my direction.

"Of course you're not." Mrs. Rollins sipped tenta-

51

tively at her drink without looking at her stepdaughter. "And that's why you're not going to behave like one. Is yours all right, Mr. Brill?" She had to keep a tight rein on herself or else under the influence she might slip into a Southern belle coquette routine.

"It's fine."

Bunny took the hint and started out.

"I'll talk to you later," I assured her. She didn't reply.

"Well, now, Mr. Brill," Yvonne Rollins said when the door had closed, "we've indulged in the amenities, and I hope you'll forgive me if I come right to the point. It's been a very trying day for me. In fact, this whole thing has been a terrible ordeal."

I waited.

"I understand Bunny's hired you to investigate my stepson's suicide."

"Not exactly. She wants me to find out why he killed himself."

"And I want you to let the matter drop. This business has been most disturbing for all involved, and I'd like it not to receive any further publicity. General Rollins has a name and a reputation that I'm obliged to consider."

"I wasn't planning on any publicity," I answered. "And it occurred to me that General Rollins' good name might be better served if his son were exonerated from his prison-camp behavior."

"I won't have it," she snapped, harder than she'd meant to. "I've no wish to be unreasonable," she added with a nervous smile," and I've no doubt you've gone to considerable trouble already, and possibly some expense. Could I reimburse you for both and have us call it quits?"

"I don't think that would make Bunny particularly happy. She very much wants to know the facts."

"Bunny is a child." She permitted herself a refined snort. "A sophisticated child in many ways, but immature in others. Surely you can see why she insists on knowing the facts, as you term them. She's looking desperately for a way to come to terms with the reality of Rollo's act. I know I'm coming on like the wicked stepmother"—she sounded genuinely unhappy about this— "but I must do what I feel is best for Bunny."

"She's of age," I pointed out. "And I'm not sure wanting to know what happened is such a bad idea, psychologically speaking."

"Have you thought of what her reaction will be when she learns? I have it on good authority—from his commanding officer—that the boy collaborated with the North Vietnamese."

"The Pentagon seemed to believe his charges to be insufficient. That leaves the truth dangling in mid-air."

She controlled herself with a visible effort and took another sip of her drink, which was going fast.

"The Pentagon wished to spare itself the adverse publicity of additional incidents of this nature."

"That remains to be seen, I'd say."

"What do you hope to get out of this?" she demanded harshly. "Forgive me, but I know your kind, Mr. Brill. I've had experience with gumshoes before. Why don't we quit haggling? I'd appreciate it if you'd name your price and let's terminate this disagreeable interview. My daughter has better things to do with her time and money than throw them out the window on a wild-goose chase."

Mrs. Rollins was possessed of hot- and cold-running charm. She had a way of speaking that suggested a carefully considered vocabulary. Similarly, her tailored clothes were designed—like the room we sat in—to provide a genteel look, a refined look. But every movement she made contradicted this structured impression. The effect jutted out at you like her breasts and threatened you.

"I think we've been over this ground before."

She stood up, flushed red and breathing heavily.

"I'm sorry you've chosen to take this attitude, Mr. Brill. I only hope you won't come to regret it."

I stood up also, having no desire to stick around for any more abuse.

"Is that a threat, Mrs. Rollins?"

"It's—it's just what I said," she faltered, angrily. "Now will you please go?" She was literally shaking with anger.

"If you like. But I promised to talk to my client."

"Your client," she sneered. "Go ahead. I don't give a good goddamn what you do. Just get out of this room."

She didn't need to invite me twice. I left her leaning against the fireplace, staring at her empty Old Fashioned glass on the mantel. They had more to say to each other.

Bunny was sitting on a bench in the foyer, looking like a patient waiting to see the dentist. She'd replaced the rebel wisp of hair.

"Want to drive me to the airport?" I asked. "I'm flying to Boston tonight to see Lewis Browne."

She brightened at once and came forward.

"What do I do with your car?"

"I don't know. Drive it back to my office and put it in the supermarket parking lot. There's a cabstand right

54

there and you can come home by taxi. Is that all right? It'll give us a chance to talk."

"Just let me get my coat."

"You're of age," I said as we started out of the drive. "Why do you let your stepmother intimidate you like that? You had every legal right to be present during our conversation."

She didn't answer for a moment, concentrating on a gap in the evening flow of traffic getting onto Sunset.

"She doesn't intimidate me. She was very upset this evening, I can't tell you, and a little drunk. I just felt I was better off humoring her."

"You've decided you can trust me."

"Please. I feel so bad about what I said at the cemetery." There was another pause for the mechanics of getting on the San Diego Freeway. "She did try to buy you off, though, didn't she?"

"Were you listening?"

"I didn't have to. She told me she would." She smiled. "Yvonne's always been honest with me—it's one of her many good qualities," she added, slightly defensive because I'd seen her stepmother tight. I decided to help by changing the subject.

"How am I going to get in touch with you?"

"I'm going to stick around home for a while. My classes break for the summer tomorrow so there's no point in going back except for my thesis research, and I can do that at UCLA. My roommate's going to pack my notes and stuff and mail them."

We drove for a stretch in silence while I made a few tentative tries at fitting pieces together. I didn't have the right pieces.

55

"She has a slight Southern accent. Where's she from?" I asked finally.

"Yvonne? Someplace in Georgia, I think. Atlanta? A real Southern belle out of Margaret Mitchell by Tennessee Williams. How come you're flying out now, at night?"

"I'm saving you money."

5 For some reason, Boston wasn't as popular a nighttime destination as Los Angeles. Or maybe it was simply the difference between a 747 and a 707. I suppose they must fill those giant freight cars on some flights, but I'd never seen it.

In the present instance I had a row all to myself, and made up my mind that when the time came I'd ask for a blanket and a pillow and sleep my way to Logan.

I wasn't sleepy yet, though. It was only ten-thirty and I wanted to look over the letters and photographs Bunny had given me. They were wrapped in a folded Manila envelope that was too large for the contents, and tied with a string as well as taped. Inside, a cardboard laundry shirt-stiffener (I wondered whose) protected the photographs. There were two of them. One was the candid I had seen on General Rollins' desk. I studied the face more closely and decided that I liked it. Maybe that was because it looked a bit like Bunny's, or maybe because it looked softer, less artificially posed, and more ingratiating than his father's.

The second picture was a kind of wire-service photo that had probably appeared in some local Los Angeles newspaper, possibly even the LA *Times*. It was a group shot of twelve men standing and kneeling before a barracks under a sign in hand-painted amateur lettering that said "Pleiku Hilton." Rollo was kneeling second from the right and smiling into the camera with the same friendly bemused expression he seemed to adopt as a habit when photographed. At the back, with his eyes partially closed as though the shutter had caught him in the midst of a blink, was Tony Bruno—his gold second-lieutenant's bars were now silver. He had the same rigid attitude held for his graduation picture and he was the only soldier with campaign ribbons and insignia showing. It's strange, but people have compulsions—or consistent indifference—about cameras. They react the same way whenever one is aimed at them, it seems. Perhaps it has to do with the primitive notion of having one's soul captured on the celluloid. In a way, Bruno's ideas about behavior before the camera were more like General Rollins' than the General's own son's. I thought of that speech in *Henry IV* where the king wishes Hal were not his son, but rather a changeling's prank that deprived him of Hotspur. Very literary. The other ten faces in the picture meant nothing to me. None of them were black so I knew I wasn't looking at Lewis Browne. At the bottom of the photograph was an identification code, which had been written on the negative in black pencil and emerged white on the print. I turned it over and on the back there was an illegible signature—probably the editor's notation—dashed off in pencil.

A short note was attached to the letters with a paper

clip: "Please take very good care of these, Mark, as they mean a great deal to me. Bunny."

I opened the first one. It was written on white letter paper and filled with a messy scrawl in smearing ball-point:

Pfc. H. Rollins
II Corps, 2nd Battalion
12th Inf. (C Company), 4th Division
Camp Enari (Pleiku), Vietnam,
Southeast Asia, The World

Feb. 3, 1969
(Tet à tête!)

Dear Bunny:

Well, here we are in guess where, and it's been about a week. Tomorrow we go "forward" to someplace or other and I may not be able to write too much there, so this is it. Just to catch you up on what happened after leaving Conway, we stayed with TWA, stopping at Oakland, then up to Washington, then someplace in Alaska (Sitka—sp?) I think. I was asleep at the time. And then on to Tokyo where we changed planes and boarded a C-130 transport, which I thought would never get off the ground. From Tokyo we flew to Long Binh (north of Saigon), where we waited for two days in pouring rain—this is the beginning of the monsoon season, as I understand it (we can expect seven more weeks or so)—for transport to Camp Enari, which is ten miles from the town of Pleiku in the heart of the Central Highlands. (Enari was the first guy who got killed here, I think.) In addition to the rain and the mud, I am suffering from alphabet soup. Everything is abbreviated and you have to learn to read your orders in a kind of gobbledygook that would make Mr. Wesley screech chalk on his blackboard.

My unit was "standing down" for a week at Enari (that means resting), but tomorrow we're off and running again. Enari isn't the worst place in the world; there's just not much to it: barracks, LZs (landing zones—for helicopters, or "choppers"), mess and clubs for officers, NCOs and enlisted men. Speaking of officers, it may interest you to know that Tony commands my platoon (I wonder who was responsible for that, ha ha), and he is now a first lt. So far we've kept a respectable distance. Most of the guys are deadheads from Alabama and crazy places like that, and they spend time bullshitting and trying to wangle jeeps into Pleiku at night for booze, broads and whatever else. They don't seem to do much in the thinking line. I'm generally regarded as weird—already—because I've been caught sketching and reading books with hard covers in my bunk. The old man (how is he, by the way?) would be thrilled if he met my only real friend. He's a spade from Boston and everyone around here treats him like shit, but he's got something on the ball. We got together when he came into barracks one evening when I was drawing. We started talking about painting, and I thought he was an ignoramus—which he is—but boy can he draw! Now, of course, everyone thinks we're queer because we sit near the barracks sketching at the end of the day instead of attending the movie, and I can tell you, it's bad enough being a queer, but when your girl friend is black, that's the lowest. Ha, ha. His name is Lewis Browne and I think you'd like him, though I must report that Tony felt obliged to talk to me about it. He did everything but ask if I'd want my sister to marry one. Good old Tony. Well, I see I'm running out of page and tomorrow is the big day. Maybe I will try to get into Pleiku for a couple of hours, after all, if it's not too late. (VD might up my status!) I'll write when I get the chance.

Cheers, Rollo.

Not a bad letter, aside from an overindulgence in parentheses. I folded it and took out the next one.

Somewhere north of Ban Me Thuot

April 1, 1969

Dear Sis:

Happy April Fool. Sorry for the long silence but we've been busy, and between you and me, that's a euphemism. Still, it's April Fool and I couldn't resist, so I am writing this to you from inside my hooch (which is a do-it-yourself tent made out of two ponchos), instead of sacking out, which is what I feel like doing after walking all day. It's getting dark, but there hasn't been so much rain lately (Thank God. I feel like I'm made of mud!) and there's plenty of light coming from rockets, flares, mortars and other assorted shit, which is pounding into our fire base right now. It's kind of like being afraid of lightning when you know it's being aimed at you. Lucky so far. (Knock wood.) I'm sorry to have been so long writing, but thanks so much for all your letters, and thank the old man for his; they really can cheer you up around here, and that's important. Since I wrote last, we were lifted by choppers called "Hueys" (or "slicks," because they land on runners instead of wheels) to brigade headquarters at Ban Me Thuot and then again by chopper to our present forward position with the battalion, in the middle of nowhere, to the north. Enari was pretty flat, with fields, meadows and stuff, but this is jungle, though not the kind in the Tarzan movies. More like really dense forest. Every day or so we go out on patrols. There's all different kinds; some are only a day or so long; others go for up to three and four days. The longer the jaunt, the fewer guys come along. But they all have one thing in common. Sooner or later they start shooting at you. Or booby-trapping you. Two days ago two guys with us got blasted to smithereens by a land mine while they were cutting point. Which was pretty hairy if you happened to be twenty paces behind them. Then we had to recover their bodies, which was messy and twice as dangerous, but I don't think I have killed anybody yet, myself. Tony is very big on patrols and goes out on them whenever he can. He's after his captain's bar and it's no big secret. What a clown. Well, that's about it. I've really got to get some shut-eye. Give my best to the old man and Yvonne—but keep the best for you, squirt.

Cheers, Rollo.

P.S. Infantrymen are called "Grunts." How about that.

Without hesitating I opened another letter.

61

Still north of Ban Me Thuot, God help us

Dear Bunny:

I'm a sergeant. That's right, honest-to-goodness stripes, though we aren't supposed to wear them out here. Well, shut my mouth, as Lew Browne says (he made sergeant, too), and won't the old man be tickled. Of course I'm only an E-5, but I could move up. Out here anything's possible. This war is as stupid and illogical as I thought it was back in the States, but we're here (because we're here because we're here), and you can get really angry at the gooks, no matter how morally right they are, when they keep trying to kill you, and sometimes succeed. I've got horror stories that keep me awake at night with the shakes and sometimes I find myself crying at the least little thing I'm so jittery. At such times I tell myself that I made sergeant. You never know when some old Vietnamese peasant or some five-year-old baby isn't packing a live grenade. The rains have picked up again after a couple of glorious months without them and I'm back to being a mud pie once more. What an Independence Day. Tony is pretty chipper; he's going to make captain any day now. Got to run; sorry if this is brief and/or disorganized, but there's a special on C rats and if I don't get them now they'll be gone.

Love, Rollo

P.S. Now I carry the radio! Details later.

And another.

Same

August 1, 1969

Dear Bunny:

Well, it's finally happened. Somebody I really cared about has been hit. You remember Lew Browne, the spade I told you about who liked to draw? Well, yesterday he was out on a sweep and got it from an AK-47 or a mortar (I'm not sure which) and he's been MEDEVACKED the hell out of here. And I didn't even get to see him. They were ambushed and had to be rescued by choppers (and one of them got shot down), and

Lew's probably in some brigade hospital by now, if he isn't in Graves. Which I don't know when I'll know. I can't tell you or expect you to understand how upset I am, but I'd really like to kill some gooks right now. He was the only halfway decent guy I've met here and now he's gone. I can only cross my fingers and hope he's okay. I've got to try and take my mind off it, I guess, or I'll go bananas. Speaking of which, Tony has put me in charge of the radio—known as the ANPRC-25 (more alphabet soup for you)—when we're out on patrols. This means I have to stay near him when he's along, which he says is the point. It's so he can report to the old man that he's keeping an eye on me. (More brownie points, even if he doesn't make captain, which he hasn't, as yet.) That's about it, I guess. I'm just too blue to write any more. Take care of yourself and keep those letters coming. And thank Yvonne for all the goodies. They were great and so was her letter. Tell her I'll write soon.

Love and X X X X X, Rollo

There were two more letters in the same vein. Mention was made of an R and R spent with Lewis Browne in Bangkok before his wound (still unspecified), and the same spirited ironic tone prevailed, though the letters were shorter and contained more description. Tony Bruno was mentioned once in each of them. He still hadn't made captain and a subtext of gleeful satisfaction crept into both references. They were quiet, absorbing letters, once you waded through Rollo's atrocious penmanship. At the bottom of the packet were some Brownie color snapshots of Vietnamese children (one of them wearing a Scarsdale High School T-shirt), and old wizened peasants. The pictures were labeled in neat block printing in their white frame margins. Enari, Ban Me Thuot, and so forth.

I put all the material back into the Manila folder, taking pains not to crush or fold anything, and sat back to consider the strange case of Harold Rollins III, dropout, soldier, wit, artist, and suicide. The pattern was not entirely unfamiliar, but there were points about Rollo's case that gave me pause. It wasn't hard to see why Bunny wanted to know what had made him do it. Although he didn't fit the conventional success-story mold—far from it—there was internal evidence that Rollo had been digging himself out from under. And yet it wouldn't do to adopt too many of Bunny's prejudices and attitudes; Rollo certainly had an unstable history, and who knew what the Swamp had done to him? He wasn't a flaming partisan of the war to begin with, and North Vietnamese prison camps had apparently turned other prisoners around, though it remained to be seen how they had managed it in each case. Margot Koontz had seen the marks on Rollo's back from his sessions with the VC.

I looked around to make sure there wasn't any other chance acquaintance who'd stolen into the seat next to mine while I'd sat absorbed in Rollo's letters and pictures. And seeing that no one had, I asked the stewardess for a blanket and a pillow, slipped off my shoes, and slept quite comfortably the rest of the way to Boston.

6 Logan had changed since I'd last been there. It had lagged far behind the airports of other major cities, and there was a time when it was nothing but temporary Quonset-hut-type buildings you could walk through from one end to the other. Time and the taxpayers had caught up with Logan and now it was quite impressive—and hot. A steamy June in the East had caught me unprepared. Stepping off the plane into the terminal building, even with its air-conditioning, was like walking into the jungles of Guam. Later I learned the air-conditioning was on the blink.

I picked up my suitcase at the baggage claim and took it to the men's room, where I extracted my shaving tackle and a clean shirt. When I'd finished shaving, I strode out to the hack stand in front of the arrivals building and got into a waiting cab. Outside the terminal, the sticky heat was even worse, and the cab was not air-conditioned. The air was laden with the salt of sea breezes, but they didn't help.

"Where to?" the driver demanded without bothering

to turn around. He had a strong New England accent.

"Just a sec, let me see." I pulled out my notebook and checked the address. "Thirteen sixty-five Pringle Avenue, Roxbury."

"Now hold on—" He turned around.

"I'm holding. Let's go."

"Mister, I ain't goin' to Roxbury, not no way—"

"It's Roxbury or citationville, Herman, we both know the law. Now come on; it's broad daylight, to put it mildly, and I don't feel like arguing."

"Couldn't you take another hack?" he whined. "Look, I'm not trying to put you on, mister. Last two times I was on Pringle I got knocked over both of 'em."

"You'll be safe with me."

"Please, have a heart, huh? My ticker ain't so good and my old lady—"

"Okay, okay." I swore in a burst of impatience and got out of the car with my suitcase. It was too hot to sit there jawing with him. I swung into the cab behind him and repeated the address. The driver, younger and long-haired, turned and inspected me through a pair of mod sunglasses.

"You sure you know where you're going?"

"I'm sure. Let's go."

"All rightaroony."

He snapped down his meter and we were off.

Roxbury isn't all bad, and it isn't as bad as it once was, but much of it isn't very pleasant, and visiting it in the steamy summer months—especially for a Caucasian—might be classified as unwise. Especially Pringle Avenue, which proved to be a broken-down street comprising pawnshops with heavy bars across their windows, so that they looked more like jails, dilapidated pool halls, unsanitary-looking short-order eateries, and barbershops that didn't appear to have cut any hair recently.

It wasn't yet noon, but the street was full of people sitting and standing like statues on tenement steps in an effort to fend off the heat. You couldn't tell the loiterers from the residents. There probably wasn't much difference.

A number of wrinkled posters pasted on crumbling brick walls advertised a film called *Ludwig the Mad King of Bavaria* and promised that "once again your eyes will be opened."

Only the children were active, sitting on or beneath open fire-hydrant spigots and splashing about. Water is a great toy. Garbage was everywhere. The driver and I were the only whites around.

Thirteen sixty-five turned out to be a walk-up tenement that looked no better or worse than those on either side of it. On the front stoop, two large ladies were fanning themselves in silence, sitting in the shadow of the building. If they reacted to my taxi they gave no outward sign.

"You don't want me to stick around, do you?" my driver asked.

"You're a big boy." I tore a twenty in half and gave him one piece. He muttered something appropriate under his breath and locked his front and back doors after I got out with my suitcase.

I started up the steps, but my path was blocked by the two large ladies.

"Excuse me."

They looked up with exaggerated slowness.

"I'm looking for Lewis Browne."

They continued to stare blankly, but behind their stares was hostile uncertainty.

"Is he here?"

One of the ladies reached down and pulled out a can of Narragansett from somewhere beside her.

"In the back. Ground."

"Thank you."

I started to squeeze by her, and for a moment she looked puzzled and indecisive. Then she shrugged and moved a fraction of an inch.

Inside the door at the top of the stoop was a tiny vestibule, painted a flaking green and permeated by the odor of urine. On one wall an ancient buzzer system had once listed the occupants of the building. A couple of cards were still there, but they were too faded to read. The rest were gone and the buzzer system didn't work. Or need to: the inside door had been removed.

I turned to check on the cab and saw that it was still there, though the driver looked unhappy; people were beginning to gather across the street, gazing in ominous idleness. I hoped money was as popular here as on the Coast, and turned down the hall. It was paved with white hexagonal tiles of the kind you find in old high-school washrooms, and littered with trash that spilled out of open garbage cans. On one wall someone had painted a large mural depicting the Boston Common on a bright summer afternoon. The picture was faded and had been defaced by spray-can graffiti indicating that Suzie sucks and Howard and Amy belong together forever. The stench was overpowering.

At the very back of the hall, past the staircase that led to the apartments above, was a single door. Beyond it, the hall ended and opened out onto a small back yard, overgrown with weeds and cluttered with more refuse. All the other tenements on the block had similar back yards, once separated from each other by fences; now most of the fences had disappeared or stood sagging and yawing and rotting, so that a strong push would have toppled them. I thought I detected some movement and stepped forward to see if children were playing. It was only rats sitting down to an early lunch.

I knocked on the door and got no answer. I knocked a second and third time and the door was finally pulled slowly open by an eight-year-old boy, who looked up at me with wide eyes.

"I'm here to see Lewis Browne." No response. "Is he your father?" He blinked. "Is he here?"

"Who that?" a voice called from within.

"Man," the boy called inarticulately over his shoulder.

"Mr. Browne?"

There was a scuffling sound and I thought I heard something fall. A moment later an enormous black man in a T-shirt and fatigue khakis limped to the door. Lewis Browne was alive, as reported, but definitely not kicking. He supported himself on a pair of aluminum crutches and his left pant leg swung freely.

"What you want?"

"To talk to you." He looked me up and down.

"You got a warrant?" I shook my head.

"Well, I don't want to talk to you, man, so—"

"It's about Rollo." He blinked.

"Rollo?"

"Harold Rollins? I heard you were bunkmates. I'm not a cop. May I come in?"

He stared at me for another moment, then gently

pushed the boy aside. "Suit yourself." And limped back without waiting to see if I'd follow. I did.

The apartment showed traces of an effort to make it habitable. It was crowded and the stuffing spilled out of the furniture in places, but the floor was tidy, except for some crayons and coloring paper. There was a new RCA color-television set in the middle of everything and a soap opera was on without the sound. On the walls were murals. An easel covered by a dropcloth with no canvas under it stood by a small sink filled with dirty dishes. An unmade single bed with an army blanket pushed to one side revealed a thin mattress covered with soiled blue-and-white ticking. Behind the bed a window with cracked, unwashed glass looked out onto the dismal back yards.

Browne hopped over to the bed and fell on it without ceremony. The child went back to his crayons and pictures on the floor, but looked up at me anxiously every so often. I sat down on an article of Sears lawn furniture with a lot of the weave missing. The room was stifling.

Browne lay on the bed, pulled the blanket absently over his arms, and leaned against the wall, watching the pretty, silent pictures on the television. Sweat rolled off him but he didn't lift his arms to wipe it. I opened my tie.

"It doesn't make any difference to me," I said, to break the ice, and pointed to his arms, which were covered with needle punctures. He turned slowly and stared at me, his eyes refocusing.

"What you want, man?" He spoke in an affected drawl.

"To talk, like I said. About Rollo."

"Ain't seen him." He turned his attention again to the television.

"Not since he got out of prison?"

He didn't bother to answer. The child now sprawled out on his belly on the floor drawing pictures. He looked up now and again at the television for subject matter, then frowned in concentration and bent over his task.

I watched Browne, who was gazing at a deodorant ad without irony. It wouldn't do to rush him. There was a protocol here that he had established and his dignity wouldn't like being pushed. Finally I decided we'd had sufficient silent communion.

"Rollo's dead. Did you know that?"

For a moment he didn't move. Then, slowly, he turned around again.

"He's dead, is he." It wasn't really a question, but in a way it was.

"He shot himself Wednesday night." I stole a glance at the boy. He didn't appear to have heard.

"No shit. Good for him." He seemed about to go back to the television again, then changed his mind. "You a friend of his?"

I shook my head.

"No, but you are. And I know his sister. She sent me to talk to you."

"What for? He leave me something in his will?"

"Could be; I don't know. She's trying to find out why he killed himself."

"Shit, how the fuck would I know why the dude did it? Maybe he wet his pants."

"All right, now, we've had our fun—"

"Who the hell do you think you are?" Browne exploded, leaping to his one foot and rotating madly on the single crutch that had been within reach. In one practical motion, he lifted the other and with the rubber-tip end poked the off-button on the television. The boy looked up at his father with shoulders hunched, waiting for the blows.

"Who the hell?" he repeated. "You bang down my door and walk your way in here and start asking a lot of no 'count questions about some dude I hardly ever saw, and when I don't answer like you want me to, you start pulling honky rank on me. Well, you listen good, honky. A man's home is his castle, you hear? His castle! An' if you start fucking aroun' in this here castle I'll kick your white ass for you to kingdom come. You ain't got no search warrant. I know my rights."

"I'm not searching for anything except the truth about Rollo," I replied. "I'm sorry if I spoke out of turn."

"You better be." Browne subsided onto the bed again. "I don't stand for no jive talk in this here castle."

"Were you hoochmates?"

"Nah, jus' in the same platoon."

"And you were friends." He shrugged with disinterest. "He wrote to his sister about you. He said you were the only decent man there."

"He said that?" His eyes showed their first spark of real interest. "How about that?" But he wasn't all that impressed.

"He said you had real talent as an artist. I can see what he meant now." I gestured toward the murals.

"Don't shit me."

"That's what he said," I insisted, without laying it on. "How come you're living like this? You get veterans' benefits, don't you. Didn't they give you a prosthesis?" For a moment I thought he was going to get angry again, but he changed his mind.

"I don't get any benefits, man."

"Why not?"

"Because this address is condemned, man, that's why not. You got to show your address when you sign up, and this ain't no address."

"Can't you move?"

"No way. I picked up a habit in Nam. I got to feed it." He held up his arms listlessly.

"And the leg?"

"Oh, they gave me one." He pointed to a box under the bed. "Only I don't like to wear it, specially when it's hot. It don't fit so good. And anyway, I ain't got no place to go."

"What kind of person was Rollo?"

"How come his sister don't know? Why don't you as' her?"

"I'm asking you. I understand you liked to sketch together."

He nodded, sort of.

"What else?"

"I don't remember."

"Did you ever go on R and R together?"

That sparked a memory.

"Hey, yeah, we did go R and R-ing together. He's only one who'd go with me." He chuckled wetly. "We did have a time."

"Where was that?"

"Bangkok, man. Bangkok. Wheeew!" He warmed to his topic. "Was that ever a town. We fucked oursels blind, and drink? We drank till we couldn't stand up—

back when I *could* stand up." He stared ruefully at his empty pant leg, coming down from the memory.

"When were you hit?"

"July '69. Mortar." He made a swooping gesture with his hand and accompanied it with a shrill whistle. "One minute it was there, the next it wasn't."

"Did you know Captain Bruno?"

"Course I knew him. Lieutenant," he corrected.

"Did you like him?"

He spat.

"Did Rollo?"

He shrugged.

"They were cousins or somethin'."

"Bruno knew Rollo's father. Did they get along?"

"Not for shit." He laughed again. "That Lieutenant Bruno, he was a regular toy sojer, you know what I'm sayin'?"

I nodded.

"All the time spit and polish. Keerist! Spit and polish in the middle of shit. Even the rest of the brass thought he was loco." There was silence. "Shot himself?"

"That's right."

Browne thought about this for a long time.

"Oh, my God." He started to cry, big tears running down his face along with the perspiration.

"I'm sorry."

"You're sorry," he mimicked, still weeping. "Oh, my God."

"Do you know any reason why he would want to? Did you hear anything about Major Bruno's charges on television?"

He wiped his eyes with the back of an enormous hand.

74

"It was on the news?"

"Yeah. Bruno accused Rollo of collaborating with the North Vietnamese. Rollo's death was reported, too."

"Well, I didn't see it! What do you want?"

"What about the charges? Do you think they might be true?"

"Nope."

"Why not?"

"I just don't. I knew Bruno and I knew Rollo, that's all. More 'n likely Bruno was doin' blow jobs on the VC and wanted to cover up." He favored me with an impish grin behind what was left of his tears.

"Was he queer?"

"You know what I mean. Rollo, he didn't give a shit about the war any more 'n I did. We didn't have nothing against gooks, you know? We didn't even know what we's there for." He leaned forward on the bed. "But when they start killin' yo' buddies an' like that, it gets you mad anyhow. Rollo wouldn't play ball with them." He seemed quite certain of this. And Rollo had expressed almost identical sentiments.

"Torture can make a man do many things," I suggested.

"You tellin' me, man. Look where it's got me. Look, maybe I'm wrong. I wasn't there. But I don't believe it. Rollo didn't look tough, but he was. Me," he reflected, "I looked real tough. But I wasn't. Shot himself," he repeated, then looked up. "With what?"

"A forty-five."

Browne broke into a toothy smile.

"A forty-five? Well, well, well." He laughed again.

"What's the joke?"

"He finally learned to use a handgun. He never did have the hang of it. He's left-handed, you know? They kept tryin' to teach him to use his right hand, but he didn't have no co-ordination, know what I mean? He could use a rifle okay, but he did have trouble with side-arms." He laughed again. "Well, I guess he licked that."

"Let me get this straight. He couldn't fire a pistol?"

"He could fire it; anyone can fire a pistol. Only with Rollo you'd have to get way out of the way." The thought continued to amuse him. "He wanted to use his right hand but it just wouldn't aim. They did have a time." He shook his head with the wonder of it. "Course a pistol ain't good for shit over there, anyhow."

"He managed to hit his temple all right."

"Looks like he did."

At this point our conversation was interrupted by the loud banging of the door at the end of the hall. There was a shriek of female laughter and the clattering of high heels on the tiles. Browne's attitude changed in an instant. He thrust himself on his crutches and elbowed past me toward the door of the apartment. But he wasn't fast enough. A key turned in the lock and the door was opened by a slim woman in her twenties, wearing a ludicrous curly blonde hairpiece and a red dress slit up one side, revealing a skinny stockinged expanse of thigh.

"I got it, I got it!" she chortled, before he reached the side of her head with the end of a crutch. Her squeals of delight changed to a yelp of pain.

"Shut up. We got company." He hobbled back and she followed in docile silence. Her face was covered with layers of make-up, the colors all starting to run to-

76

gether in the heat. She looked like a painted totem pole, but underneath I thought she might be very pretty.

"I was just leaving."

"No hurry." She favored me with a wide grin and her tired body automatically straightened into a provocative posture, which strained the seams of her tiny dress.

"Shut up," Browne repeated. He came toward me and accompanied me to the door. Behind him, I saw the woman shrug wearily and bend down to fondle the boy, who stretched up his arms in her direction.

At the door, Browne plucked me by the sleeve. His features fought with each other, pride, fear, hunger, and anger struggling for expression.

"You said something about a will," he reminded me, dropping his accent.

"Here's something on account." I opened my wallet and gave him a hundred dollars. He tried to act casual. "Let me give you a piece of friendly advice," I added. He felt obliged to humor me. "Get yourself and your lady to a methadone center on the double. Then move out of here and sign up for your benefits. If you don't, all three of you are going to go down the drain without a trace." It was easy to say.

"Yeah, yeah," he agreed hastily, "I'll do that. We sure are grateful." He was still mumbling hypocrisies as he cut himself off by closing the door in my face. As I walked down the hall, I could hear yips of happiness emanating from Browne's apartment. He was having a good day. And if Bunny thought a hundred was too much, I'd shell out fifty of his compensation on my own.

Outside, the sun was beating down as though it meant to boil your blood, and my cab was nowhere to be seen.

The two ladies were still fanning themselves and working on what I now saw was a case of Narragansett. They hadn't moved back after letting me pass, so I was able to edge my way by and down the steps. As I did so, one of them muttered an obscenity behind me. I wasn't about to take her up on it.

There were plenty of folks sitting on other stoops and not all of them looked so harmless. In fact, two of them were getting up to say hello to me. I couldn't really blame my driver for chickening out.

He hadn't though. As I tensed for the approach of the two blacks, the cab screeched around the corner and pulled up in front of me. He unlocked my door, I threw my suitcase in and followed it, and we squealed off. Money talked, after all. I sat back with a sigh of relief. I know when I'm outmatched.

"Bet you thought I split." He grinned at me in the mirror.

"Bet I did."

"Nah. They were getting kind of edgy so I just kept going around the block. Bad for the old gas tank, but good for survival."

I handed him the other half of the twenty, said I'd give him extra for the gas, and told him to take me back to Logan.

"That's it? In and out, just like that?"

"Just like that."

"You're missing the best of Boston," he protested.

"Where's that?"

"Cambridge. I'm into sociology at Harvard."

"Then you're missing the best part," I muttered.

At Logan, I decided I was hungry. The air-conditioning had been fixed and was now operating double time to make life bearable for the people inside. It was almost chilly and I chose to take advantage of it and eat before I grabbed the Eastern shuttle for New York.

Before I entered the restaurant I stopped at a phone booth, looked up the methadone center, and told them about Lewis Browne. They weren't in the prosecuting business, and it did seem like a damn shame for a man with a Bronze Star and a Purple Heart to rot in Roxbury. Browne might hate me for it, but just possibly he wouldn't.

7 By three-thirty or so I should have landed at La Guardia and been on my way into New York, but as we flew south it started to rain and all hell broke loose. It was a Saturday afternoon and everybody wanted to land at La Guardia, which left us in a holding pattern at twenty thousand feet for an hour, after which we inched our way down, the rain getting heavier all the time. The airport itself was a scene of damp confusion and I had to wait another ten minutes to get a phone booth to myself.

I called Dr. Fairfield's home and got his answering service, which informed me that he was out and asked in friendly but brisk New Yorkese if they could have the doctor call me.

"Do you know where I might reach him?" I countered. "At the hospital, say? It's rather urgent."

"Are you a patient?"

"No."

"Well, we're not permitted to give out that information. If you'd care to leave word, I'll see to it that the doctor gets the message." She sounded genuinely apologetic.

I told her my name and said I'd booked a room at the Holiday Inn on West Fifty-seventh Street and would be there in an hour.

That proved to be an understatement. Grand Central Parkway was bumper to bumper and but for the ingenuity of my cab driver—who got off it and took me through some back streets and alleyways of Queens—I wonder when I'd ever have checked in.

I arrived at about seven and found no message from Dr. Fairfield, so I called again. The answering service said he was out for the evening. Under pressure, the girl told me that he made Sunday morning rounds at Sinai. I promised I wouldn't betray my source. I'd used that line about a rare blood type being run to earth before and it was hard to resist, especially when neither of you knew what you were talking about.

Then I sat back on my comfortable double bed and looked out the window at the dusty twilight and continuing downpour. New York on a Saturday night in June and me all dressed up with no place to go.

I decided to call Penny Klein, an old flame of mine who worked at CBS News. She'd produced a documentary a few years back that purported to take a look at real-life private detectives—I think it was called *The Real Private Eyes*—and I started out as a segment. The finished film came close to winning an Emmy, but I didn't find it particularly interesting. I did find Penny interesting, and almost succeeded in winning her. She gave her age as thirty-five—and almost looked it—had been married once and divorced, and was generally the black sheep of a blue-blooded Newport dynasty who'd given up all hope on her long ago. Our relationship had declined to fits and starts but we usually had a good time.

Her apartment didn't answer, which left three possibilities. Either she was on a date, stuck somewhere in rainy transit, or still at her office. The third possibility was one I wouldn't put past her, though I wasn't too hopeful. I called CBS and asked for Mrs. Klein. After a moment's hesitation the switchboard's dial was answered by a secretary who announced: "Penelope Wordsworth." It took me a second to realize she'd gone back to using her maiden name.

"Could I speak with Miss Wordsworth please?"

"She's very busy at the moment; could I have her get back to you?" I breathed a sigh of relief.

"Just tell her Mark Brill is on the line before I hang up, will you?"

"Mark Brill. Just a minute." She put me on hold long enough for me to grab a cigarette and light it.

"Well, Mark, for Christ's sake, what an awful trick to play." Penny's voice came chortling through the rain. "Where are you?"

"In awful New York. I've just come from awful Los Angeles by way of awful Boston. How are you, Penny?"

"Ragged at the edges." She didn't sound ragged. "This Watergate business is going to make or break me. How are you?"

"I'm fine. As a matter of fact, I was just in awful Washington, testifying at a trial."

"Not you, too," she gasped.

"Have dinner with me and I'll tell you all about it."

"Oh, Mark, I just couldn't. I'm up to my ears and I've already canceled out on a very eligible party. How long will you be in town before you jet off again?"

"This may be it, cutie. How about making an exception?"

"Gee." I could picture her at her desk, eying mountains of paper work with a thick editor's pencil stuck in her straight black hair and her glasses sliding down the ridge of her nose. "I really shouldn't."

"You may be missing something really important," I teased. "Besides, doing things you shouldn't can be fun."

"You are an awful man. All right, give me some time to finish here, get home and change. Say—" she stopped to check her watch—"quarter to nine?"

"I'll be there."

"I'm terrible."

"That's what I like about you."

We hung up and I unpacked, shaved, and treated myself to a long hot shower and some thoughts about Harold Rollins. I'd now heard from two intimate witnesses. Anything they said about the Swamp would be hearsay, but neither of them believed Rollo was a collaborator. One admittedly had no idea how rough the VC could be, but she had seen Rollo's scars. If that's the way they want to play, that's fine with me, Margot Koontz had quoted him when he'd learned of Major Bruno's charges. She'd described him as elated rather than frightened. Lewis Browne hadn't been in prison with Rollo, but he'd served with him and known him well enough for Rollo to describe him as a friend. Getting a statement from

Browne had been like drawing teeth, but his views had amounted to the same thing. And what was all that about Rollo's being unable to use a pistol with his right hand? He shot himself in the right temple, which probably isn't very hard even if you do have right-handed troubles, but on the other hand (no pun intended), isn't it more likely in that moment of stress that the suicide performs automatically with the hand that is most convenient? Or was his use of the right hand some kind of ritualistic celebration in which he felt he had to conform to military rulebooks? Or was I running amuck?

I had to stop and remind myself that I had not been hired to delve into Rollo's suicide, only its motivations. But then, I could investigate his motivations only if he had indeed . . .

My mind was going around in circles, and I decided to give it a rest on this Sabbath eve and hope that Dr. Jacob Fairfield could fill in the missing pieces. Otherwise I'd have to start checking all those names Pete Ericson was rounding up for me, and that was going to cost Bunny a good deal of money. If Dr. Fairfield couldn't play a convincing devil's advocate and Bunny was satisfied, the conclusion would be that Rollo had talked to his stepmother, and his panic over an impending court-martial—whether he was guilty or not—had simply got the best of him and he found that he couldn't face the possibility of the humiliation and the likelihood of another jail sentence.

I found that I couldn't believe that. It didn't sound like any part of Rollo that I'd come to know, either through his letters, his sister, his fiancée, or his wartime heroin-addicted buddy. Rollo bounced back. He was

84

digging himself out from under. Getting his act together, as Bunny'd put it.

I really had to give it a rest.

"You lied to me," Penny Wordsworth pouted over the dinner table after I'd told her the real reason I'd been in Washington. We were sitting in an unpretentious French restaurant on East Thirty-fifth Street that was kind of naughty, but naughty and nice. The lights were the sort that wouldn't be affected by a power failure and the service was unobtrusive. Penny, I realized, had been there before, though that shouldn't have meant anything to me. She was wearing a white silk summer cocktail dress, with almost no back and a plunging neckline in the front, which added up to an enchanting structural impossibility.

"I don't get to doll myself up like this very often," she said, catching my admiring glance.

"Now who's lying? Incidentally, how long have you been using your maiden name?"

"Almost a year. Just when I was getting tired of Klein I discovered women's lib and figured what the hell. I kind of like it." She continued to smile happily and I went on ogling.

"Has it hurt your career?"

"It's caused some confusion—especially at first," she admitted.

"And probably kept you off the enemies' list," I added.

"Do you know any way to get me on?" She leaned forward eagerly, putting down her fork. "It might make all the difference."

I said I didn't and asked her what the truth was concerning Watergate. The waiter arrived and discreetly absconded with the remnants of our *coq au vin*. I asked her about Watergate again over brandy.

"I only know what I read in the papers, chum."

"That isn't exactly saying much for television, is it? Someday we'll look back on all this and laugh," I predicted.

"After Richard's been crowned it will all seem like a bad dream," she agreed, solemnly. "What brings you to New York? It's your turn now."

"Did you do a story on Sergeant Rollins and the charges filed against him by Major Bruno?"

"Rollins." She thought a moment. "Rollins. Of course. That was only this week. You were putting me on. We do remember this week, you know."

"Well, that's why I'm here," I said, and told her the details.

"Isn't he going into politics now?" she said when I had finished.

"He who?"

"Major Bruno. I seem to remember a follow-up about his leaving the Army and running for Congress somewhere around San Jose."

"It's news to me," I confessed with interest. "What are his chances?"

"San Jose's as right as you can get in the north of California. If my memory serves he's going in as a Republican to try and fill Masters' seat when he retires at the end of his term. He's a war hero and a POW, and his charges brought him some kind of national notoriety.

That's always good for 'name recognition,' according to politicians. He might stand a chance."

"Even though his charges were dismissed by the Pentagon and resulted in a suicide?"

"Name recognition; national notoriety. That's the name of the game, chum."

"Where did you get this 'chum' business? I don't think it's very nice."

"I'm sorry. Force of habit, I guess. When you're in an institution dominated by male chauvinists, it's easy to slip into their jargon. Protective coloration. If I don't sound like a woman I guess maybe they'll pay attention to what I'm saying."

"But you do sound like a woman. And you look like one." I reached out for her hand across the table. "And I am listening to what you're saying."

"Which brings us to our next point." She stared candidly into my eyes. "Your place or mine?"

"How do you feel about the Holiday Inn?"

"Yecch. How do you feel about East Seventy-third Street?"

"Why don't you ask me when we get there?" The check arrived and I put it between us. "Now whose expense account is going to pay for this?"

"Yours," she said, stubbing out a cigarette. "I'm not as liberated as all that."

We stepped outside under the awning, and let the doorman get wet finding us a taxi.

Later we lay still in her bed and listened to the rain trying to be heard through the air-conditioning.

"Why didn't I marry you?" She turned and looked

at me, lying on her back, her eyes glistening, hair spilled out on the pillow.

"You wouldn't come to LA." I reached for a cigarette in my jacket pocket on the chair of her dressing table.

"That isn't it, and you know it. How much longer are you going to be a detective? A private detective." Her lips curled in gentle scorn. "My God, Mark, that's just so—so immature."

"Who told you that, your analyst?"

"He didn't need to," she responded with a sigh. "If there's one thing I learned from that documentary it was the transparent regression involved in the psyches of private eyes. You're all hyped on Action comics and Paul Newman movies."

"Ohhh." I clutched my side. "You got me right where I live, doctor."

"Be serious." She rolled over on her side and nibbled at my ear to show me how serious she was. "You can't spend your whole life chasing after other people's dirty laundry."

"It seems to be good enough for the President," I pointed out.

"That's just my point. There are so many things you could do, Mark. Real things."

"Such as?" I was trying not to get depressed. We'd had this conversation twice before and it was beginning to feel like an instant replay.

"Oh, I don't know. Be a reporter." She sat up, excited with the thought. "Sure, why not? You've got the investigative part nailed down—"

"Now all I need is a degree in journalism."

"I could help you by-pass all that," she said impatiently, grabbing my cigarette and taking a drag. "It's all Who What Why Where When and How. And don't worry about your English," she added brightly. "It doesn't count for anything these days."

"Penny, I am not worried about my English. I am worried about this conversation."

"Sorry," she said glumly, and proceeded to prove it. It seemed almost worth it. Here she was, beautiful, loving, and intelligent, and here I was, aging and getting lonelier. I turned off her arguments because I really didn't have any answers or, at any rate, reasons I could articulate. Action comics. My God! Was that really what I thought about my job, deep down? Maybe I should head for the couch.

"Hey." Penny was sitting up with the sheet wrapped around her and her chin propped in her hands.

"Hey, what?"

"It's probably nothing, but I just thought of something. I mean I think I thought of something."

"This sounds fascinating. What?"

"About your Major Bruno. I knew his name had a familiar ring, even before this week." She clapped a hand to her brow. "Now what the hell was it?"

"You were going to tell me."

"It was a couple of years back," she said hesitantly, "and it wasn't directly about him, at least I don't think it was. But he was part of it."

"Can't you do any better than that?"

"I'm trying, damn it, but I was going through my divorce, and everything in that time frame is always through a pair of sunglasses darkly. Give me a minute."

I gave her a minute but nothing happened.

"I'll never get to sleep now," she protested, unwilling to give up the subject.

"Who said anything about sleep?"

"Too bad you didn't call me in advance," she whispered, snuggling into my arms. "You could have padded your hotel bill."

"Too bad," I agreed.

Afterward, we did sleep.

The next morning when I woke up, Penny had already gone downstairs, picked up a Sunday New York *Times,* and stopped at her neighborhood delicatessen. By the time I had made some passes at my face with a Lady Remington and stepped out of the shower, the kitchen table was covered with lox, bagels, cream cheese, and other assorted goodies.

"Come and wallow in it," Penny said.

"Is this supposed to be some kind of inducement? Preview of coming attractions?"

"When you're in New York, the whole world is Jewish. Something my parents could never understand," she added, half to herself. I sat down, checking my watch. The big breakfast made me uneasy, but I couldn't tell if it was because I had an appointment to keep or felt threatened by Penny's domesticity.

"Don't eat so fast," she cautioned, restraining my bagel-holding hand. "You want to give yourself an ulcer or something?"

"Something. I told you I had an appointment this morning."

"But that was last night," she protested, eyes widening. "No one has appointments on Sunday morning in New York. It's a tradition."

"One I'll have to break, I'm afraid. This guy's difficult to pin down—"

"I'm not," she interrupted, pouring coffee with a smile. Her smile was strained. She had lots of spirit but it was wearing thin. She didn't want me to go. I couldn't tell whether I wanted to or not. Fortunately or otherwise, the choice was out of my hands.

"He's making his rounds this morning and if I don't catch him I'll have to sit it out until Monday or maybe longer."

"Would that be so terrible?" she chided.

"Maybe not for me," I admitted. "But my client would have to pay for it and her resources are not unlimited."

"Oh, it's a *her*." Penny was engaged in studiously spreading cream cheese over her bagel.

"Now cut that out."

"Sorry."

"And stop being sorry. You have every right to be annoyed. Frankly, I don't see why you put up with a louse like me."

"You don't?" She looked up, her eyes very bright.

I left shortly after, promising to call when I was finished. After the lox and cream cheese, it felt appropriate to be going up to Sinai to get the word.

8 The previous night's downpour had tapered off to a muggy drizzle as I made my way up to Mount Sinai Hospital by cab. It took some doing to locate Dr. Fairfield, owing partially to an error in my information. Fairfield was no longer a surgeon but a hematologist. I had tried catching up with him for more than a mile of corridors when a nurse advised me that I could head him off at the cafeteria, where he usually stopped for coffee at about this time. I had to thread more labyrinth to locate the cafeteria, which was half filled with medical personnel, none of whom appeared to enjoy Sunday morning rounds. Groups in white sat in subdued clusters, rubbing their eyes and grimacing over the hospital's version of coffee.

Two doctors on their way out pointed to a prematurely bald young man seated by himself and identified him as Fairfield. He had a tray with scrambled eggs, coffee, and tomato juice on it, and he was eating and drinking listlessly, as though he were bored or fatigued, or both. A pair of steel-rimmed glasses rested on the top of his head, their lenses dealing glancing blows to the fluorescent lighting. Next to him, but folded, was part of the Sunday *Times*.

"Dr. Fairfield?"

"Yes?" He looked up in mild surprise with soft-brown vacant eyes.

"My name is Brill. I've been trying to reach you."

"Brill," he echoed, more or less to himself. "Oh, yes." He jerked his head so that his glasses fell into place over the bridge of his large nose. "You called my service and told them some strange story about looking for a rare blood type? What was all that about?"

"Nothing," I confessed. "I want to talk to you about Sergeant Rollins. May I sit down?"

"Sergeant—? Oh, I see. Are you a reporter?"

"Yes." I reported to somebody. He still hadn't offered me a chair, but he seemed lost in thought over my statement, so I helped myself.

"Actually, I've been thinking quite a bit about Sergeant Rollins," he admitted, still appearing to address himself. "I've just been reading in the News of the Week in Review about his suicide."

"And?"

"And?" He shrugged and went back to his food. "It's a terrible business. Terrible. And shocking."

"Why shocking?"

"Well, his killing himself. It was so—unexpected. I guess it usually is."

"You didn't think of him as the type?"

"Well—" There was a pause as Fairfield tried to envisage Rollo as the type. "No, I guess I didn't."

"What about Major Bruno's charges?"

"What about them? I must confess they took me by surprise. Would you like some coffee or something to eat?" he asked solicitously, coming out of his reverie. "I can't promise that it's very good. And I'm sorry about the Muzak."

I explained that I had eaten and asked him how he came to be at the Swamp.

"That's rather a long story." He spoke with exasperating slowness in a rhythm that made you want to finish his sentences for him.

"I'd like the highlights if you'd care to give them to me." I reached into my breast pocket and took out my notebook and pencil. He eyed them with a new frown of puzzlement.

"Are you going to use this in your article?"

"I might."

"Well." He patted his mouth with a paper napkin and began searching his white coat pockets for cigarettes. I offered him one of mine. "No thanks. Those are much too strong."

"The surgeon general has determined . . ." I smiled and handed him a light.

"It's hard to quit," he observed reflectively, taking a long drag.

"You were going to tell me—"

"Oh, yes. I'm sorry. I guess I'm always a little vague on Sunday mornings. Vaguer than usual, perhaps."

"I understand."

"I was in my second year of residency at Deaconess —you know Deaconess?" he interrupted himself.

"In Boston, isn't it?"

"That's right. The Navy asked me to volunteer as a

navy doctor. They were willing to pay for the rest of my residency, and it was either that or enlist or be drafted, so I figured what the hell." He put down his cigarette and took a swallow of tomato juice. "They sent me to Camp Pendleton for two weeks along with a bunch of other doctors and dentists, and we went through a crash program to turn us into navy doctors. Two weeks!" He laughed with quiet disbelief. "Then they shipped us to a marine base over in I Corps, near Saravane. Know where that is?"

"Roughly."

"And presto, we were all second-lieutenant navy doctors. For six months I worked in *triage* there, operating sometimes around the clock on the wounded as they were brought in by the choppers. Sometimes there were ten, sometimes a hundred. You never knew, and they were shot up every which way—you never saw anything like it," he muttered. "Nineteen- and twenty-year-old boys with legs, arms, hands, feet, and sometimes even their heads shot off. Men in their prime, and for the life of me I couldn't figure out why. We never knew what happened to them after we worked on them, either," he added, as though this were the worst part. "We'd spend three to six hours trying to save some kid's life and never know if he made it or not. The choppers would pick them up and take them to Saigon—or home—out of our lives. Some doctors thought it was better that way, but I don't. If I spend my time and energy—and I'm talking about emotional energy, too, understand— if I spend time and energy trying to save a man's life, I want to know if I succeed or not. It's important to me. But we never did."

"The Swamp," I reminded him.

"Oh, yes, the Swamp. Well." He pushed his glasses onto the top of his head again and leaned back, looking at the ceiling and thinking. "Did you ever hear of an operation called Medical Civilian Aid Program?"

"I don't think so."

"Lucky you. It was some highfalutin notion of the government for making friends and influencing people, specifically, our Vietnamese allies. Once a week a group of corpsmen—sometimes with a physician along, but most often not—would leave the base under marine escort and visit some of the outlying, supposedly friendly Vietnamese villages. There they'd distribute trinkets among the natives. You know—malaria pills, tetracycline for VD, snakebite kits, aspirin, isoniazid, Kool-Aid, cookies, and candy. The folks didn't seem to care what they got as long as they got something. They probably passed the good stuff on to the VC.

"Well, one Saturday—the MEDCAPs were usually held on Saturdays—the CO asked me if I'd go along. I think it was so he could report that a doctor had volunteered from his unit and have it on his record. And I, filled with the idealism of the whole thing—helping the people we were supposed to be there helping and all—I said sure. And that's how it happened. One minute I was looking at a six-year-old girl with a typical case of malnutrition and the next I was in the hands of the VC —and so was everyone else. I don't know what happened to the corpsmen and the squad of Marines who were with me, but I guess they killed them. They didn't have the men or facilities to take a lot of prisoners, but a doctor was useful. They took me and the contents of

96

the medical mobile unit we had with us and bingo, there went five years out of my life. It could have been worse, I suppose." He was thinking of the dead Marines.

"Was it usual for a *surgeon* to go out on MEDCAP?"

"Never heard of it, myself. Usually they wanted internists. But I guess no one was in the mood that morning. And that was the end of my career as a surgeon," he added, holding up his hands. They quivered slightly. I hadn't noticed.

"They took you to the Swamp?"

"Not at first. This particular patrol was based in a rubber plantation that was French owned, I think. All I know is the artillery had orders not to shell it because it cost them fifty bucks for every tree they destroyed. So it made a perfect place for them to hole up. They had that plantation honeycombed like a rabbit warren with men, supplies, facilities. There must have been five hundred NVA operating out of that rubber plantation. Fifty bucks. What a war."

"And prisoners?"

"Not many. They didn't have that kind of room or foodstuffs. They used it as a kind of way station for transporting us farther north. There were maybe twenty of us there."

"For how long?"

"A week, maybe two or three. I find it hard to remember some things."

"Well, there's no need to dwell on them. Then they moved you up to the Swamp?"

He nodded.

"When did you get there?"

"Oh, June—mid-June, 1969. That place made the rubber plantation look like the Waldorf Astoria."

"How did you meet Sergeant Rollins?"

"In the usual way. They brought him in like the others. They made me the camp health officer, so I checked everyone when they came in. Another laugh." He didn't laugh.

"And Lieutenant Bruno?"

"Him, too. He got promoted to captain while he was there. That was good for another laugh."

"How did you become friends with Sergeant Rollins?"

"Coincidence, I guess you'd call it. One of the boys who slept in my hut—hut is a charitable description, you understand—this boy died the night before. Ruptured appendix turned gangrenous and I didn't have the equipment to save him. Name was John Dowe, pronounced Doe, if you can believe. Anyway, he died and Rollo took the vacant spot. It wasn't too popular because being around the quote, health officer, unquote, you saw and smelled a lot of things that didn't help your sleep. Rollo didn't mind. In fact, he became my assistant."

"How did he seem when he arrived?"

"Exhausted, emaciated, feeble, and jumpy. He had nightmares."

"Did he ever talk in his sleep? Use phrases like 'Stop the killing'?"

He looked at me with surprise.

"Where'd you hear that?"

"From his fiancée. Did he?"

"Not at first. At first he just couldn't sleep at all. In fact, that was one of his major problems."

"What about Lieutenant Bruno? What kind of relationship did he have with Sergeant Rollins?"

Fairfield thought a moment. He was a good witness—slow, undramatic, but scrupulous.

"One-sided," he declared at last.

"In what way?"

"Well, one of the reasons Rollo decided to room with me—if the prison commandant would permit it, which he did—was to get clear of Bruno."

"He told you that?"

"More or less. Not in so many words. But I had the impression that he didn't like Bruno or, at any rate, didn't want to talk to him."

"Did Bruno want to talk with Sergeant Rollins?"

"All the time—at first. Whenever he could wangle it during exercise period or medical check, he tried to get Rollo aside and have a few words. Rollo didn't seem to like the idea. I remember one time . . ." He trailed off.

"Yes?"

"It was strange. I guess you could say I was eavesdropping, though I hadn't meant to. I was sacked out in the hut one afternoon, and they either didn't see me or didn't think I was awake. I *was* only half awake, but I recall coming around to the sound of voices. It was Sunday and they didn't have us doing anything—unless you wanted to hear the army chaplain we had, which nobody much did. Anyway, I found I was listening to a conversation between Bruno and Rollo about six feet away from me."

"You're sure it was them?"

"Oh, quite sure. Bruno's voice was hard to miss. I don't know if you've heard it on the news recently, but it's a kind of nasal monotone and rather high-pitched for a man his size and build. Incongruous, if you know what I mean. And besides, the question's academic because I saw them after a while."

"What were they saying?"

He eyed me suspiciously.

"Are you sure this is for your paper?"

"It's for my story. I'm free-lancing at the moment, and Sergeant Rollins' suicide interests me very much. It means a great deal to me."

"To me, too. Well, where was I? Oh, I came out of this semidoze I was in and heard them talking. Bruno seemed to be asking for something. He was saying something like 'Can't we come to some sort of agreement on this?' and Rollo was telling him that he needed more time to think about it. Then Bruno went on about the importance of reaching an understanding, and Rollo said what was so important about it now, and Bruno went into some speech I couldn't hear too much of about duty and honor and Rollo's parents, and Rollo told him to cut the crap."

"Then what happened?"

"Then I sat up and asked if they would cut the crap also, because I was trying to get some shut-eye."

"Are you sure you've got this the right way around? It wasn't Sergeant Rollins asking Lieutenant Bruno if they could come to some agreement?"

He looked at me with dormant indignation.

"It was just what I said. Bruno was asking Rollo. I remember it quite clearly. God knows why."

"Sorry. I didn't mean to challenge your recollection

of events. What was the reaction when you asked them to tone it down?"

"They both seemed a little embarrassed. Bruno more than Rollo, as I remember it. Rollo just said, 'Sure thing, Jake,' or words to that effect, and lay down to get some rest himself."

"And the lieutenant?"

"He acted kind of flustered and kept apologizing for disturbing me and hoping it was all right and more stuff like that. I told him it was all right only would he kindly get lost since it was too hot and damp to waste our energy talking when we could be sleeping. He said okay, okay, okay, several times like that, placating kind of, and got his ass out of there."

"Did you ever ask Sergeant Rollins what that conversation had been about?"

"Nope. I didn't have much curiosity about anything by that time. Would you excuse me while I get another cup of coffee? I've got to get back in five minutes."

"Maybe I'll join you."

"Suit yourself." He scraped his chair back and I followed him to the coffee machine at the end of the food line. Through an open window I could see the bus boys scraping the garbage and plastic flatware indiscriminately from hundreds of used trays.

"Did it ever occur to you that they might have been discussing some escape plan?" I asked as I filled a Styrofoam cup.

"Nope. For the simple reason that nobody escaped from the Swamp, or even bothered trying. Did you ever see that movie *Bridge on the River Kwai?* Well, that's kind of what it was like. No fences, no guard towers or anything like that. Just the swamp and the prison itself, which sat on a high bank of sand in the middle of it. The VC had built a single-access causeway, but they patrolled it night and day. A regular tropical Alcatraz."

"Just a couple more questions," I said, glancing back over my notes when we returned to our table. "About Bruno's charges. You say they took you by surprise. Why is that?"

He lit another cigarette.

"Because I didn't know anything about any collaboration. And being around him so much you'd think I would have. Certainly more than Bruno, who was way the hell on the other side of the island." He leaned forward. "Look, if a guy collaborates or plays ball with the North Vietnamese or the VC, I don't care which"—he forestalled me with an impatient gesture—"it's to get something in return. Special privileges, more chow, less work—you name it. They didn't give Rollo any of those things. To the contrary."

"What do you mean, the contrary?"

"Rollo had it in for them. It seems they'd shot up a particular friend of his—I don't know much about it because Rollo didn't say much—but Rollo couldn't do enough to get in their way. Once he told the camp interpreter to tell the commandant he was ready to film an antiwar propaganda statement for them. They were always trying to get us to co-operate about things like that. Well, they went to a great deal of trouble, got a film crew down from Hanoi or somewhere and set everything up—and then Rollo refused to say a word. Can you imagine? They went ape, the commandant probably shit in his pants when he found out Rollo wouldn't talk.

It put him in very bad with his superiors when he had to send back that camera crew empty-handed. Course he took it out of Rollo's hide. But Rollo knew they would. They dumped him in solitary, stopped feeding him, and drummed assorted patterns on his back and buttocks with some kind of hose. I protested and threw the Geneva Convention in their faces but they were just too hopping mad. Rollo just took it in stride. He said he was letting them expiate his sins for him, or something like that. They had him in solitary a lot. Sometimes I think I taught him more about medicine using his own body as a lab specimen than any other way, but that was fine with him. In fact, he started to sleep better."

"Sometimes when they've got a man in solitary, he co-operates and no one's ever the wiser," I suggested.

"I suppose that's possible," Fairfield conceded reluctantly. "For all I know, he talked his head off."

"But you don't think so."

His eyes met mine. They weren't vague any more.

"No I don't."

"Did the Pentagon check with you on any of this?" I asked, getting to my feet.

"Yup. And I told them. Hell, the camera-crew story was common knowledge all over the camp. It helped boost our morale. Rollo was a kind of hero."

"But I gather you didn't mention the conversation you overheard between Sergeant Rollins and Lieutenant Bruno."

He looked surprised.

"They didn't ask me. And I didn't figure it was important. Is it?"

"I wouldn't know. What did you think of Lieutenant Bruno?"

"Didn't know him worth a damn. Is that all? When will I read your story?" He stood up and started piling things absently onto his tray.

"I don't know that, either. I'll have to see if anyone wants to run it."

"I sure hope someone does. That boy was screwed."

"It looks like maybe he was," I agreed, and said good-by.

When I got to the Holiday Inn, which as yet I hadn't really used, I called Penny and asked if she'd care to join me there for a few hours before my plane left.

"You mean for a quickie? Thanks, but no thanks. I'm sitting here looking at a bunch of stale bagels and thinking I've been had, Mark."

"I'm sorry, but I do have to get back. I wanted you to be had again is all."

"I don't think so."

"Penny, I'm really sorry."

"I hear you telling me. Oh, what the hell. We had fun, didn't we?"

"That we did."

"And who knows? I may get out to sunny California yet."

"I wish you would. Oh, by the way, did you ever remember what it was about Major Bruno that occurred to you last night?"

"Not yet, but I'm working on it. I'll call you if I do."

"Please. I'd really appreciate it."

"You can count on me," she said dully and we hung up.

Then I placed a long-distance collect call to myself in California. I had an arrangement with my service. If I had any messages of importance they accepted. There was only one message but it had been repeated several times so they put me through. Bunny Rollins had called six times. I told them next time she phoned to say I was on my way.

I got to Kennedy without incident and returned to Los Angeles with only throbbing pangs of guilt. One of these days Penny Wordsworth was going to get tired of being a good little soldier, and I wouldn't be able to blame her.

9 I got back to Los Angeles after midnight Sunday (really very early Monday), suffering from jet lag, a bad conscience, and the continual replaying in my head of my nocturnal exchange with Penny about the adolescent motivations that kept me at my profession. Give it up and she was as good as mine. What was it, anyway, this private-eye routine? Fifteen years on the force and another ten chasing after—what had she called it?—other people's dirty laundry. She made it sound pretty damn juvenile. Was I really a slightly more mature version of E. Howard Hunt, rattling cloaks and daggers in a closet? A closet rattler. A dirty laundry rattler. And was it all so dear to my heart that I couldn't give it up? For a lovely woman like that, whose only crime—to hear her tell it—was that she wanted me to act my age, in return for which she had virtually offered to be the companion of my declining years?

I had no better answers for these questions than I'd had in New York, except that I had developed an inkling over the past three thousand miles that I didn't really want to know the answers.

Why? I was tackling this one as I unpacked my suitcase and piled up laundry (laundry again) beside my bed, and deciding that it was too late and I was too tired to give it a decent go, when my phone rang. It was Bunny.

"I've got to see you. Now."

"Now? It's pretty late. Can't it wait?" I sat down on the edge of my bed, sagging.

"No, it can't. I tried to reach you all Saturday. It's very important."

I looked at my watch. It was almost one in the morning.

"All right. Where shall we meet?"

"Right here. You've got to pick me up."

"Pick you up? Bunny, why can't we—?"

"Please, Mark. I wouldn't ask you to if it wasn't important. I'll be waiting downstairs and watching for your car," she added and hung up.

I stayed slumped on the shoulder of the mattress for several minutes, then heaved myself aloft and threw on a jacket. At least it wasn't muggy enough to use a machete out here. I went downstairs and got into my car again and put the top down. It wasn't a wise move because the canvas was getting too old to play games with, but I figured maybe the night air would revive me.

Bunny was waiting as she'd promised, and the moment I drove up, she was out of the house and sliding onto the seat next to me.

"What's the big deal?" I demanded.

"Let's just go someplace where we can talk and I'll

tell you the big deal," she said in the same clipped nervous accents she'd used on the phone. She was fumbling badly with a cigarette.

"All right, let's go to my office."

"No! I mean, no, let's go someplace else."

"My apartment?"

She shook her head.

"Isn't there someplace public? An all-night hamburger stand or something?"

"I know a place in Van Nuys," I answered facetiously. "Would you like to go there?"

"Van Nuys is fine."

"Bunny, this is—"

"Please. Please, Mark. Just do as I say." She gave a feeble imitation of what was supposed to be a reassuring smile.

So we got onto the San Diego going north and went into the valley, getting off at Victory Boulevard and driving three-quarters of a mile east to a Denny's I knew that stayed open for twenty-four hours. Bunny was wearing her hair down—it came below her shoulders—and the wind was making a mess of it.

"You should have told me we'd be driving with the top down on this thing," she complained, searching her purse for a rubber band. "I'd have worn a scarf."

"That can't be the extent of your problems," I countered.

"Believe me, it isn't."

We drove in silence, except for her occasional injunctions to slow down, which made me angrier than anything else she'd done so far. I was at that overtired stage when I was likely to lose my temper over trifles.

"Now will you please tell me what's going on? Why all the drama?" I demanded when we'd seated ourselves at a vacant booth and ordered snacks and coffee. The only other people in the restaurant were young valley matrons, with their hair in curlers half covered by loud scarves, sitting together and gossiping quietly, and truckers eating by themselves at the counter, chewing their food like cud and staring dumbly into space. I felt like them.

"First tell me your news and then I'll tell you mine." Bunny glanced around the restaurant incuriously. I was too tired to argue with her, so I summed up my meetings with Lewis Browne and Jacob Fairfield, and included the tidbit I'd learned from Penny, namely that Tony Bruno was leaving or had already left the Army and planned to run for Congress.

"I know," she answered, distracted. "Tell me, what are your conclusions, if you have any? About Rollo."

"Well, they're tentative," I temporized, trying to collect my thoughts and sound alert. "But on the face of it, there seems to be very little evidence, in fact no evidence so far, that your brother collaborated with the North Vietnamese, or behaved in any way that I can construe as dishonorable or even questionable. Here are your letters, by the way. They were a big help." I took them out of my jacket and handed them over. She didn't look at them, but continued staring intently at me.

"Meaning?"

"Well, that's a little more difficult. One possible inference to be drawn is that Rollo killed himself because he couldn't go through the publicity and the humiliation, or that he didn't want to flirt with a military court-martial, innocent though he felt himself to be."

"Is that your conviction?" Her eyes, really more gray than blue at the moment, burned brightly into mine. It was impossible to break the spell of that stare and start in on my sandwich.

"I'm not very happy with it," I said frankly. "It doesn't seem to fit what I've learned about your brother any more than if I'd found he was a collaborator."

"What were you going to recommend?"

"That was going to be up to you." I managed to unlock my eyes and reach for my coffee. "You might want to continue the investigation, or you might be satisfied with my services at this point, which indicate that Rollo did not collaborate, and that if he killed himself, he did it out of fear, not guilt. If we continue, of course, that runs into more money."

"If he killed himself?" She repeated my words, almost through clenched teeth. "Did you say *if?*"

"Did I?" I was more tired than I thought. "I'm not sure what I meant by that. I am very tired."

"Maybe this will wake you up and provide some food for thought." She reached into her purse, pulled out a business envelope, and handed it to me across the Formica. "I got this in the mail Saturday morning." The envelope was a plain white stationer's product with Shelly Rollins' name and address typed on it and a slightly crooked eight-cent Lincoln stamp. The postmark showed that it had been mailed on Friday afternoon from North Hollywood. I opened it and took out a single sheet of typing paper.

Dear Miss Rollins:

For your own health and welfare, it is strongly suggested that you withdraw your private investigator from the inquiry into your brother's unfortunate suicide. If you persist in this reckless course of action, you will have only yourself to blame for the consequences that befall.

It was signed "A Friend."

"You got this Saturday?" I held it up to the light, looking for the watermark.

"And I've been trying to call you ever since. Oh, Jesus, you don't know how scared I've been! And that's not all." She leaned over and clutched my wrist. "This afternoon I got a phone call." She said it in a way that told me it was the same kind of communication. "Mark, it was awful. Whoever it was had this ghastly stutter. I don't know what to do. You've got to help me. This is scaring me out of my mind."

"All right, take it easy. I *am* helping you. That's what I get paid for, remember?"

"But I didn't think it was going to be like this," she protested, talking in a furious whisper and looking over her shoulder anxiously. "I didn't think there was any— I don't even know what to call it—funny business. I didn't think there was any funny business involved. Mark, you've got to tell me what to do. Should I call you off?"

"Were you planning to? If I said there was no evidence, would that have satisfied you—if you hadn't received the letter and the call?"

"Look, let's not talk academically, if you don't mind. I'm trying to find out if I'm supposed to be afraid for my life. Now come on!"

"What did he say, the voice?"

111

"The same thing. Asked me if I'd gotten the letter and then went into the same spiel."

"Using the same words?"

"Yes—no—hell, I don't remember—"

"Well, think. It might be important." And give her something to do instead of indulging in a rising tide of panic.

"Uh—he said, 'Miss Rollins?' And I said yes, not really thinking what this was going to be. And then he said, 'Miss Rollins, I hope you've received our letter and given it careful consideration—' "

"Our? He said *our?*"

She nodded.

"Then he said something about it would be a shame if anything happened to a nice young girl like me, with a future ahead of her, and stuff like that—"

"And he stuttered throughout this whole thing?"

"Real bad. Sometimes he could hardly get the words out. I waited for him to finish," she concluded mournfully, and then looked up again. "Do you think we should go to the police?"

"That's a good question. We might, of course. That letter constitutes some kind of threat, and so does the phone conversation, though we have only your word for that—"

"You don't believe me?" Her eyes began to widen.

"That's not the point. We're talking about what the cops would have to go on. What time was the call, by the way?"

"About two this afternoon."

"Did you tell your mother about it? Or the letter?"

She shook her head.

112

"I didn't want to upset her. And I knew that if I did, she'd only use it as an excuse to insist that I call you off."

"That implies that without her insistence you weren't planning to."

She stopped and gaped.

"Does it? Yes, I suppose it does. But what about the police?" she repeated. I sat back and thought. "Now you can understand why I was afraid to leave the house by myself or go to your apartment or your office," she went on while she waited for me to finish thinking. "I thought how awful it would be—when I couldn't get in touch with you—if they killed me simply because I hadn't been able to fire you."

"You could have left word that my services were no longer required," I pointed out, waking up at last and examining the letter again. "That seems to bear out my original thesis that you really don't want me to stop. This letter certainly makes use of a strange vocabulary. Very stilted, wouldn't you say?"

"We were talking about bringing in the police," Bunny reminded me. "Do you or don't you think it's a good idea?"

"It depends what you want them to do. If you want to be guarded round the clock for a while they'll do fine. But they won't find out what happened to Rollo. The clues are cold, the body's likewise, and the case is closed. They aren't going to find any prints on that letter or the envelope. They'll point out the high incidence of crank mail after sensational events of this sort and argue that the letter makes no claim to the authorship of your brother's death. They'll give you lip service, but that's all. And I'll bet my bottom dollar the FBI won't touch it, either," I added, before she could ask me.

"But supposing we let the police do what you say they would—guard me or whatever—while you stay on the case?" she asked with timid ingenuity. "Wouldn't that—?"

"Think about what you're asking. We'd get in each other's way in no time, and all the while whoever it is that sent this will be watching you. And if they mean business, the kind of protection the cops can offer won't help. Christ, even the President isn't bulletproof and you know what kind of precautions they take. The moment you call in the cops, that's when they'll really get tough. The cops'll get tired or bored or careless and that may be the ball game. In any case, they can't keep watch over you forever. That costs money and they've got more important things to do—from their point of view," I amended.

She'd been leaning forward. Now she sank back on the cushions of the booth with something like a sigh and began playing aimlessly with the spoon in her cold coffee.

"So your advice is to leave the cops out of it."

"For the time being. We can always call them in if we really need them."

"Or if we're dead."

"Or if we're dead. But if you ask for them now, you're not going to find out about Rollo and you'll probably be aggravating the danger to yourself. You could do nothing," I went on. She looked at me. "Fire me and drop the whole thing. Then they'd probably retreat into the woodwork and you'd be left alone. How much does it mean to you to find out about Rollo?"

"I used to think it meant a lot." She winced. "But that was before I knew that I might be risking my own neck in the process. I'm not the stuff of which martyrs are made." She allowed herself a little laugh. Her hair looked very nice, framing her face in gold.

"No one's saying you have to be."

"Do you think I should forget it? Don't give me some line that'll make you a couple of hundred more. I'll pay you an extra two days to give me an honest answer."

"I'll give you the honest answer free. I don't think you're the kind of person who can leave something like this half finished. It's obvious that some forces have been brought to bear on your brother's death that aren't as simple as you at first supposed. And if you were willing to clear his name I think you're up for clearing the rest of this, too."

"But I'm afraid—"

"And so am I. We'd be nitwits if we weren't. You'll have to stick around the house and not go out unless you're with your stepmother, and never at night. It won't be easy and it might not even be safe, but that's the chance you'll have to take if you feel strongly enough to want the answers."

"I want them," she admitted. "What about you?"

"Me?" Her question took me by surprise. I thought she was more involved in her own problems at the moment. "I've made it so far. I'll take my chances, too, I guess."

"My brother may have been murdered in that den,

115

isn't that true?" She latched her laser eyes on to my wave length again.

"Yes."

"That doesn't sound to me as though the house is too safe."

I thought about this.

"Stay out of the den," I told her, and drove her home. On the way back, we elaborated on safety precautions for Bunny, including regular checking-in hours for me, more specific do's and don't's for her (including not going down the drive to the mailbox, a habit of hers when she was at home), and ways in which she could reach me that my service would act on immediately.

"What's your next move?" she asked, after I'd drawn up to the front door of her house.

"You mean after I get some sleep? I'm going to start working this case from the other end."

"Meaning?"

"I'll stay in touch. Let's not get in the habit of blow-by-blow descriptions."

"All right." She took a step closer and looked up at me shyly in the waning light of the moon. "Mark. Thank you."

"I'm only—"

"I know," she said hastily, "but thank you. Anyway."

"You're welcome. Anyway."

I waited until I heard the lock click in the door before starting the engine and heading home.

As I unlocked my apartment door, I could hear the phone ringing inside. A cold sweat broke out almost at once and I dropped the key. Could something have happened to her already? I was nuts to have left her alone, nuts to have given her that bullshit about toughing it out.

"Hello, Bunny? Are you all right?"

"M-m-mister B-b-b-rill?" The voice was hoarse and breathing fast. So was I.

"This is Mark Brill."

"J-j-just a f-f-friendly w-w-w-w-word of ad-v-vice, M-m-mister B-b-brill. S-stay off the R-r-rollins c-c-case, if you-you-you know w-w-what's g-g-good for you. S-s-somebody c-c-could get h-h-hurt."

"Now listen—"

But there was a click and no one was listening. It was a weird voice and the stutter was so bad it sounded either phony or unintentionally comic.

But in my heart I knew it was the real thing.

10 I woke up after only four hours' sleep and felt more refreshed than I'd expected. An attempt to trace the previous night's mystery-phone-call threat had come to nothing, which didn't surprise me, and no solutions came to me in my dreams.

But I woke up with a strong hunch that my luck with this case was about to turn and that starting from the other end was all I needed to get the ball rolling.

Starting from the other end simply meant Tony Bruno. The more I looked into Rollo's death—I no longer felt justified in referring to it as a suicide, even if subsequent circumstances were to prove that his finger had been on the trigger—the more Anthony Joseph Bruno, career officer, hero, All-American Boy Wonder, and would-be Congressman, began to stink to high heaven.

I called Bunny as per our checkup schedule, but didn't tell her about hearing from the stutterer. Then I got in my car and drove over to the campus of LA Civic University and started asking questions. I told

118

people I was a reporter gathering background information on Bruno for a magazine, and this did not seem strange to them. Tony Bruno's alma mater was proud of his congressional aspirations and eager to be of help. LA Civic was a municipal land-grant college boasting an enrollment of some fifty-five hundred students, most of them from the Los Angeles–Orange counties area. It wasn't what you would call a sophisticated seat of learning, but it was accredited, and the dean, a fussy roly-poly type who poked you with his finger when he spoke, for emphasis, pointed with pride to the number of graduates in high-paying jobs.

"And you know how tough the job market is these days." The dean stabbed me in the chest with a pudgy forefinger.

Yes, Tony Bruno had graduated in 1968. Yes, he had been on the Dean's List. Yes, his major had been in communications, but of course he had been dedicated to serving his country and that had led to his increasing involvement with the college's ROTC program. Of course the program had been discontinued, and the Brigadier (as he insisted on referring to General Rollins) was now unhappily deceased, but if I wanted information, I might contact Capt. Walker Brisbane, who'd had Tony in his classes. And where might I find the captain? No problem, no problem at all, the dean would just check his files and was sure he could tell me where the captain was now in residence. The captain was back at Camp Conway, south of LA. I copied down the address, got into my car, and headed for Conway, a half hour down the relatively traffic-free San Diego Freeway.

Captain Brisbane's wife, an attractive woman in early middle age who bore an appealing resemblance to Pat Nixon, informed me in pleasant accents that the captain was out on the golf course, and that if I cared to I might run him to ground there. "Run him to ground" were her words.

I drove to the golf course and located the captain in the company of several other officers, all occupied around the eighth hole. The captain, a mild-mannered type with horn-rimmed nearsighted glasses, gave up his game to chat with me about Bruno, recalling him fondly. There was no doubt in the captain's mind that Bruno was qualified to run for Congress, "though of course, this uniform does not permit me to discuss Tony's politics in any further detail." I harrumphed, "Of course, of course."

"That boy had a big thing about self-improvement," the captain assured me. "For example. Did you know he once had the most terrible Southern accent? No? Oh, it was just awful. When I first knew him it was almost impossible to understand a word he was saying—he was born in Georgia, you know—but damned if that kid didn't take all sorts of courses in speech therapy and rhetoric and clean up his pronunciation until you'd never know he hailed from the South. Would you have?"

I agreed with Captain Brisbane that you'd never know it.

"How did Tony spend his spare time?" I wondered. "Where did he hang out after hours?"

"That I couldn't tell you, sir." Brisbane came as close to winking as he could. "There was a bar called

120

'The Barracks' near the campus. It was very popular with a lot of my boys, I know. There was an OCS training center near it during the war, which is how it got its name. You might ask in there. I know you won't be telling tales out of school in your article." He tried winking again.

"We're all human." I smiled back and asked him for the address. The captain resumed his game.

Back toward the campus and a bar called The Barracks and decorated like one. The place brought back memories entirely unconnected with the case. The bartender, who informed me that he was " 'Sarge' to everyone," didn't react to Tony Bruno's name (except that he seemed to remember it on the news recently), or to the newspaper pictures I showed of Bruno. One showed him four days ago reacting at a press conference to Rollo's death (the speech I'd heard on the radio in my office) and the other was a reproduction of his graduation photograph, the one I'd seen on General Rollins' desk.

"Where else do the kids hang out around here?" I asked. He gave me a list of bars and restaurants that formed the nucleus of off-campus social life. I spent most of the afternoon checking them and going through my reporter routine. It didn't seem to be doing me much good. Any good. No one recognized Tony Bruno by name or photograph, except for those who associated him with his recent newspaper appearances in connection with Sergeant Rollins' death and his political plans. Some had heard he was a graduate of LA Civic. No one claimed to have laid eyes on him in their establishment.

I had worked my way to the last place on my list, a

121

discothèque that bordered the outskirts of Venice, and was starting to doubt my hunch of the morning, with all its bright promise. Tony Bruno's dean and teachers were proud and fond of him. He was an asset to the college, ambitious, thrifty, hard-working. All in all, a regular boy scout. Who apparently never touched a drop or a woman.

As I started out of the last bar Tony had never been inside of, my eye was caught by a sign across the street. It identified the place as the "Dixie Cup—House of Swing." I asked the manager of the discothèque about it.

"It don't cut into my trade," he responded, joining me at the window and looking across the street. "It means what it says, too; not what you think it says."

"How's that?"

"I mean it ain't a sex club or anything. They play jazz there, you dig? Old-time Dixie Land stuff. The kids don't go for it; it's mostly for older folks. That's why it don't cut in on my business, like I said. The kids dig rock."

I started to get my hunch feeling again, very strong. Something about Tony Bruno's stern high-sideburned look told me he didn't like rock. Rock, at least in Tony's days at school, was anti-Establishment and smacked of drugs and other illicit pleasures. I could picture Rollo and rock, but not Tony. Tony was all for the Establishment. (Tony was an anal retentive, I'd decided, and rock was for letting it all hang out.) And he was a Southern boy who had once had an accent you could cut with a knife. Was it possible that he went for squaresville?

It was only across the street.

122

The Dixie Cup was doing a brisker business than any of the other places I'd been to, which claimed they didn't get going till dark. Or maybe it was just later than I thought by the time I walked in. The place was decorated in Jezebel red, and although the bandstand was empty this early, King Oliver was coming out loud and clear over the speaker system. No one was using the dance floor; in fact there weren't too many women there at the moment, but a cluster of white-collar business types were gathered at the bar, putting it away.

The bartender was a diminutive bald gent in his fifties, who sported a pencil-thin gigolo mustache and wore a red-and-white-striped shirt that matched the décor. He wore suspenders, too, and a straw boating hat hung on a hook behind him. Above the hat, hanging down over the tops of the many bottles all standing in bleary array, an enormous Confederate flag completed the picture of the Dixie Cup.

I was forty-eight years old but the place made me uncomfortable.

"What'll it be?" The bartender mopped his way over to where I was sitting at the end of the bar and sized me up discreetly.

"Scotch on the rocks and more King Oliver."

"You got it," he smiled. "Management pays for the jukebox. Just take your pick and press the button."

"Thanks. I will."

While he threw together my Scotch, I walked over to the jukebox, an appropriately old-fashioned item in excellent repair, complete with bubbles circulating in colored glass—red and green and yellow—and told it to lay some Benny Goodman on me when King had finished. I hoped it wouldn't be considered too gauche; but then Goodman was on tap, so he couldn't be completely out of line.

"This place really swings," I told the bartender, when we reunited over my drink. "Friend of mine told me to come here and I'm glad I did."

"Oh, yeah?"

"Yeah, you probably know him. Tony Bruno?"

"Bruno, Bruno." He cupped his weak chin in the crevice between his thumb and index finger and thought about it, propping his bent elbow with the other hand. "No, gee, no, can't say as I do. Course I can't keep track of all the names." He was still trying to be helpful and maybe sell me another Scotch.

"He's been in the news recently," I said with enthusiasm. "Maybe you saw his picture." And I drew out my clippings.

"Oh, yeah. *Yeah!*" He bent over them with unfeigned interest. "My God, so that's Tony Bruno, huh? Christ, he's been comin' here for years. You know somethin'? I saw them pictures in the paper the other day and I said, Jesus, that guy looks familiar, know what I mean? I almost had him pegged, but I guess I just didn't think it could be the same guy, him running for Congress and all. And of course the uniform threw me."

"Never saw him in uniform, huh?"

"Unh-unh." He kept staring at the photos. "Jesus, that's really something. Ten years I've known that guy and I couldn't connect him."

"Ten years? I didn't realize Tony'd been coming here that long."

"Well, maybe not that long. He used to be in here a

lot say—oh—" he rubbed his chin again—"maybe five, six years ago. Once or twice a week he'd show up, usually in the afternoons, with that older broad, you know the one I mean? Then he disappeared and I didn't see him. I guess that's when he was in Nam and bein' a POW and all—"

"Wait a minute," I interrupted, plastering a grin on my face. "What older broad? Tony never let on he was hanging out here with a broad. Who was she?"

"Christ, I don't know, but she was a looker. I like 'em a little older, myself," he confided. "Older and with lots up top." He winked. "You know what I mean? And this broad was stacked. She wasn't all that old, either, or she didn't look it. And I don't know how she kept her shape with all that drinking." He shook his head. "She still looks pretty good. Maybe it's all that exercise." He made a descriptive gesture with his hands. "They always left in one helluva hurry."

"Have you seen them recently?"

"Oh, yeah, they were in the other day. Tuesday, I think it was. Yeah, last Tuesday. She still looks like a great lay if you ask me. Maybe even better."

"Well, well, well. Old Tony's been holding out on me. Let me have another Scotch, will you?

"Must be a long-time romance if they've stuck together all this time," I mused when he returned. "Jesus"—I borrowed a phrase from his book—"can you beat that?"

"Hey." He leaned conspiratorially over the bartop. "You don't want to go blabbing around about any of this, you know. Guy's running for Congress and all. It could be embarrassing, know what I mean?"

"Don't worry." I smiled and allowed my speech to slur a little bit. "You don't have to worry. Me and Tony, we're pals. I'm not gonna louse him up. I just can't get over it is all. Last Tuesday." I shook my head again at the wonder of it.

"Well, you wanna be careful," he insisted with authority. "Those politicians got to watch every step they take—"

"Hey, hey. Come here," I interrupted with a confidential wave of my hand and an assumption of what I hoped was a roguish expression. "I think maybe I know this broad. What did she look like?"

"Stacked, like I said." He tried to draw back from my hand that circled his neck with firm affection.

"That's no good. Tony always liked 'em stacked. Come on, pal, this is strictly between you and me. I just think maybe I know her."

After a moment's hesitation for further appraisal, he fell into the spirit of the thing. He wasn't a bartender for nothing.

"Well, let's see. She got red hair. Reddest hair you ever saw, and not orange, either, real red, though maybe it isn't real, if you know what I mean. I mean she must be forty-five if she's a day. And big green eyes. Oh, Christ, I'd love to tumble into the hay with that. Big green eyes," he repeated and I let him go.

"I think it's the same broad," I said enthusiastically. "You ever hear what he called her?"

"Lemme think. I think I must've once or twice, but it was some kind of offbeat name, you know? Edith?" He tried it out. "No, it wasn't Edith—"

126

"Yvonne?" I suggested quietly.

He clapped his hands with a snap.

"Yvonne, right, you got it. Yvonne. What a broad. You know her, huh?"

"Not as well as I thought," I confessed, and wound down our talk.

Driving back to my office, I started fiddling with my new pieces and was pleased to find that a couple of them fit, or might with a little juggling. At thirty-five, when Yvonne Rollins had married the Brigadier General, she was playing around with one of his cadets. And she was still playing around. Maybe that was why Bruno hung out at the house so much. Had Rollo stumbled onto it? Was that the "understanding" Bruno had wanted so badly to reach? But why in POW camp? How had it come up then? Had he started riding Rollo and had Rollo then turned around and confronted him with it? That was possible. Rollo's father was still alive in 1969 and the whole thing could've been very sticky for Bruno, if and when they ever got released.

It sounded good, especially the part about Rollo's getting fed up with Bruno's sanctimonious clean-cut hypocrisy, but I wasn't sure. There were other pieces in view on the board that demanded to fit. Bruno's once notorious Southern accent, so adroitly ditched before entering public life. Born in Georgia? Wasn't Yvonne from Atlanta according to Bunny? Was that a coincidence? Something that brought them together when they first were introduced by General Rollins? Dixie Cup camaraderie.

Or was there more to it than that? And where the

hell did the stutterer come in? Just thinking of him almost made me smile. He was right out of a very old Hitchcock film.

It was after six when I arrived back at my office, and a heavy layer of smog was stinging my eyes badly. Also, I wasn't used to putting away two straight Scotches on an empty stomach. But what really made me feel peculiar was an empty squad car parked in front of my building entrance. As I walked by and started up the stairs, I told myself that it just happened to be there, but when I stepped into my outer office and saw two policemen looking at my old magazines, I knew the coincidence was over.

"Mark?" The taller of the two cops rose and extended his hand. He and I were old friends from my days on the force. He was a craggy homicide captain named Welch, who worked hard and played poker the same way.

"Hi, Steve, what's up?" I took off my jacket and set it on the edge of a chair.

"We were hoping you might tell us." The second cop rose and smiled tightly. He was in his twenties, painfully thin to have made the force, eager for action, and his skin was pitted with old acne scars.

"Mark, this is Eric Sanderson." We shook hands in a perfunctory way and I sat down on one of my chairs. "Do you know a woman named Margot Koontz, K-o-o-n-t-z?" He checked his notes.

"Suppose I do?"

"You don't any more," Sanderson informed me, doing his best, I thought, to imitate Jack Webb. "She was shot and killed in her apartment this afternoon at about four o'clock."

"Shot?" I looked from one to the other of them, for lack of anything better, while I stalled long enough to think.

"With what looks like a small handgun, thirty-six caliber." Sanderson glared down at me. "You know anything about it? You asked to see the coroner's report on her boy friend."

"Steve, can't you ask your pal to wait outside?"

Welch shook his head and sat down across from me.

"How about it, Mark? We spoke with the girl's sister. She was at the movies when it happened, but she mentioned your name and said you'd been to see her sister last Friday. Is that true?"

"Yep."

"What for?"

"I thought she was cute."

"Now hold it—" Sanderson cut in, but Welch motioned him to keep quiet. He turned and faced me with a tired smile.

"Mark, we're trying to investigate a murder and you've got to play ball—"

"Not without consulting my principal, I'm not."

"Shelly Rollins?"

"I suppose the sister told you I'd mentioned her name?"

"You got it," Sanderson threw in. More silence while we surveyed each other.

"How about it, Mark?"

"I can tell you this much." I got up. "I don't know

anything about Margot Koontz's death, less than you do, I'm sure. I've spent the day on the road."

"Which road?"

"The San Diego Freeway, sonny. Want to see my driver's license? I've got witnesses," I told Welch before his sidekick exploded. Welch got to his feet.

"Do you know anyone who had a reason to kill her?"

"No." This wasn't really true. I found I was able to construct a theory with astonishing ease. Welch heaved a sigh.

"All right. Get in touch with your client and then come down and make a statement, will you?" I nodded. "Come on, Eric."

"So long," I said sweetly as he walked by me.

When they had gone, I called Bunny and asked her if she'd heard what happened.

"The police called and told me. Now what do we do? I'm scared out of my wits."

"Sit tight. Does your mother know? What was her reaction?"

"She answered the phone. She was very upset. She's in bed now with a slight fever and Dr. Carstairs is on his way over to have a look at her. I think she needs a sedative."

"Let me ask you something that may not seem especially relevant. What's your stepmother's maiden name?"

"Page. Why?"

"Just curious. Okay, here's what we're going to do. I'm going down to the station now and give them a statement. I'll try to keep it as uncluttered as possible, but I may have to tell them more than I'd like. You sit tight with your mother and I'll get back to you, probably to-morrow. Okay?"

"Okay." She didn't sound too happy about any of it. "I suppose it's too late now to call a halt to any of this, isn't it?"

"Yes. It is."

11 I picked up the phone again and started to dial information for Atlanta, Georgia, then thought better of it. The Hall of Records would certainly be closed at this hour on the East Coast; besides which, I didn't want to learn anything I might have to tell Steve Welch downtown. I'd get on the phone first thing in the morning.

I was in the act of putting my jacket back on when somebody knocked on the door.

"It's open." I bet it was that sappy cop, back with a parting monologue.

Nobody opened the door so I went to oblige and found myself staring into the snub-nosed muzzle of a Webley .36 caliber. It so dominated the doorway that it took a moment or two before I could shift my eyes from the gun to the man behind it. He was tall enough and wide enough to be a tackle for the Rams, but the huge steel hook he sported in place of his other hand told me they wouldn't be likely to accept him. Next to him was a somewhat shorter individual with a ragged

132

Viva Zapata mustache, a patch over one eye, and a cane over one arm. Altogether a startling pair.

"M-m-move b-b-back ins-s-side, p-please, M-m-mister B-brill," One-eye instructed, talking with a familiar speech impediment.

"And be so good as to raise your hands," added the pistol-packer with the hook. He had dictated the letter.

"You gents want to tell me what this is all about?" I asked, obeying their instructions in slow, careful movements. The one with the cane used it to push closed the door behind us. They must have waited until they were sure the police had gone.

"We've communicated that already," said Hook. He glanced quickly around the office, never lowering the pistol.

"A-a-and you-you-you've ch-chosen t-t-t-to ignore our w-w-w-warnings. You-you-you and M-m-miss R-rollins."

"We aren't interested in aggravating the situation, Mr. Brill, but apparently neither you nor your client is willing to listen to the voice of reason."

"Are you sure you've checked this maneuver out with the Major?" I inquired politely. My hands were getting tired sitting in the air. They looked at each other uncertainly, caught off guard, and I made my move, diving into Hook, coming up under his Webley, and hoping I could knock him over backward before One-eye used his cane.

I wasn't fast enough. One-eye caught me on the ear, hard, and Hook fell over backward but didn't let go of the gun. I came down on top of him, exerting all my strength on his left forearm so he couldn't pull off my face with that thing, but I'd lost my moment of surprise and knew I couldn't win. As I struggled to pin Hook's gun and hook to the floor, One-eye lit into the back of my head and neck with the cane.

In the midst of it all, my phone started to ring. One of the blows from the cane hit a nerve or vertebra or something and I lost my grip. In another instant, Hook had rolled over on top of me and rapped his steel knuckles where I parted my hair. It knocked the fight out of me and he took advantage of the respite in our exercise to haul himself to his feet and hand the pistol to One-eye.

"Boy are you dumb," he informed me, dropping the two-dollar words from his vocabulary. I'd wondered what it would take.

He walked over to the phone, which was still trying to tell us something, and brought the tip of his hook down between the outlet unit and the plaster wall. My contact with the outside world was severed in a burst of Beaverboard and a sprouting of colored wires. Any nasty ringing that continued could only be coming from one place.

"I wish you weren't making this so hard." Hook squatted down and eyed me with professional interest. His beady eyes, sunk in folds of flesh, reminded me somehow of the hole in his gun.

"You want me to drop the case? That's what you want?"

"Listen, we don't want to do this. Can't you believe us?" He spoke earnestly, and despite my recent experiences, I was tempted to believe his tone. "Rollo shot himself, we're not putting you on. We'd just rather you didn't look into it, that's all."

"Because of what else I might learn?" I tried sitting up, but his hook came out and gently nudged me to remain prone.

"More or less. Let's not go into it, shall we?"

"All right, let's not. Can I sit up now?"

"No tricks?"

"No tricks."

He waited a moment longer, then withdrew his steel fingers and stood up.

"H-h-how c-c-can w-w-we l-let him g-g-go?" One-eye protested anxiously, handing over the gun.

"We're going to come to an understanding."

"W-with h-him? You m-must b-b-be c-crazy. D-don't you-you se-see? Once w-w-we l-let him g-g-go, w-what's to k-keep him f-from t-t-taking up wh-where he-he-he left off?"

Hook frowned as he considered this view and I realized by the successive expressions on his face that he was coming around to it. But as long as he was absorbed with the pros and cons, I decided to pass the time by going for his ankles.

This time the gun did go flying, though it did not discharge, and all three of us wound up rolling back and forth on my dusty linoleum. I didn't manage to stay in the ring as long as I had the first time. One-eye held my arms over my head while Hook stuck his knee in my chest and gasped down at me, spittle forming at the corners of his mouth.

"Now you're gonna get it," he prophesied. He started to hit me, in the belly, on my chest, my face. Pounding was more like it. I couldn't breathe, I couldn't see, and blood was trickling down from somewhere onto my chin.

I couldn't tell if it began at my nose or my mouth. And I was beginning not to care. Dimly, I knew rather than saw Hook clamber to his feet. A dull thudding began on my right side, caused, I sensed, by a large shoe or boot. I wondered how many it would take to crack one of my ribs and if I'd be alive when it happened.

So long as he didn't use that damn hook. That was the only stimulus I was capable of responding to. Anything but that, like they say in the war movies. War movies. When was the last time I'd seen a good war picture? There was *Bridge on the River Kwai*, of course, but had that been recently? And wasn't it all Englishmen or something? No, wait, there was Bill Holden. Good old Bill. As American as apple pie.

The thudding had left my ribs and was working its way north, pulverizing my shoulders. I tried to lift up my head to avoid the last stop, and then, to coin a phrase, everything went black. And they were right: you do see stars.

I was playing tennis somewhere on a blindingly bright court. The court was so bright that I couldn't even see the ball jet over the net toward me. But somehow I always managed to hit it. I knew that I was hitting it because of the rhythmic *thwack thwack* the ball made when it struck my racket and then went back to be hit by my unseen opponent's. I could hear my breath, coming in gasps and wheezes as I struggled to keep up with the ball. Then mists, like that phony dry-ice effect they use sometimes in stage productions, floated past and the *thwack thwack* sounds of the tennis ball receded into some indescribable distance.

It was terribly dark. I could not tell if it was dark

because it was night or because I was in a very long tunnel or deep cave. The presence of faint echoes suggested a cave. Mysterious black shapes were flying around in the darkness, brushing my face with the tips of their wings and making soft snickering noises. Bats. They must be bats. And those noises I heard were their radar beams bouncing off the walls of my underground cavern. I thought I heard someone call my name. They must have been miles away. "Mark, for heaven's sake. It's only up to Bakersfield. I'm not that bad a driver. I'll be back by dinnertime tomorrow night." Then silence and rest. Or was it my rest that was silence?

What was I looking at now? A corner. That was it. A corner in a ceiling someplace. A white ceiling. Slowly, my eyes traveled down from the corner. Fluorescent lights. I let my eyes wander down the wall from the lights and saw a window. It was day, somewhere. There was blue sky with a familiar brown tint to it.

Right from the window. A face. A face peering anxiously down at me, with the sunlight refracted by a golden halo. An angel?

"Mark? How are you feeling?" A hand placed on my brow.

"Who's that?"

"Try to speak more clearly. I can't understand you."

"Who's that?"

"It's me. Me, Bunny. Can you hear me?"

"I can hear you. Where am I?" I tried to turn my head.

"No, don't do that. I mean you're not supposed to move your head. You're in UCLA Medical Center."

"What time is it?"

"What?"

"I said what time is it?"

"It's ten o'clock in the morning. You're going to be okay."

"Ten o'clock? You mean I've been here all night?"

"All night and all day and all night. It's Wednesday. They brought you in Monday night."

"Wednesday? No, look, you don't—is there any water? I'm thirsty."

"I'll get you some. Just lie there quietly."

I lay there quietly, trying to figure out what had happened. There was a trickle and a gurgle and then someone was propping up my head and pouring lukewarm water down my throat. It was hard to swallow at first. Then it did wonders. My eyes began to focus.

"How'd I get here?"

"I called an ambulance. See, after I spoke to you I tried calling you back. I guess I was still scared and I wanted to ask you what you thought I should tell the police. There was some kind of funny pop on the line after a couple of rings and then it was dead. I didn't think it could be out of order because I'd just spoken to you, so I checked with the operator. She said it seemed that it *was* out of order. I was so jittery that I was sure someone had pulled your phone out of the wall. So I disobeyed instructions and came to see. They had. And you were lying on the floor in a pool of blood, no less. It wasn't one of my finer moments."

"Or mine." I was beginning to remember. "You came over by yourself? What about your instructions? You could've—"

"Now take it easy. Nothing happened. I went down-

138

stairs and used the phone booth at the supermarket and called an ambulance. And here we are."

"I see." I started to prop myself up and Bunny tried to force me back down again, but I wasn't having any. "All right, all right, a ministering angel thou. Now let me get comfortable."

"You're not supposed to—"

"Can it," I ordered without ceremony. "What's my condition?"

"You've got two fractured ribs, a minor concussion—with stitches to go with it—and assorted cuts and bruises."

I felt my face gingerly and was surprised to find it felt unlike my own. It was all puffy, and there were cuts or weals or something dividing my cheeks into furrows.

"And you have a black eye."

"Can I have a cigarette?"

"Well," she responded uncertainly, "that's against the rules here, too—"

"Bunny, have a heart, will you?"

"Okay. Just don't tell anyone where you got it."

"I'd die first. Come on."

She lit a cigarette and put it in my mouth. Like the water, it had the effect of clearing away the cobwebs.

"Where are the cops?"

"Downtown, where cops always are. They're waiting for you to come around before questioning you."

"Well, I'm not going to be here. Listen, Bunny, I want you to get me a phone."

"A phone?"

"Yes, a phone. Quick. And—who's he?" I gestured

to a white cloth divider that was drawn around another bed. Bunny shrugged and looked embarrassed.

"I don't know. I couldn't get you into a private room."

"My insurance doesn't even cover this."

"That's all right. It's on me." I started to protest but she held up a hand. "We'll put it down to expenses if you like."

"Okay, okay. Just get me a phone, will you? I think this is starting to break."

"You may be the one who's starting to break," she replied. "There's a phone on the table next to you."

So there was. I picked up the receiver and asked for an outside line. I called CBS in New York and asked for Penny Wordsworth, and told them to tell her it was Mark Brill.

"I've been trying to reach you since Monday night," Penny said at the other end of the line, her old spirits seemingly restored. "Your office phone is out of order, your home phone doesn't answer, and your answering service says they don't know where you are. Are you all right?"

"I'm all right. It's just that I—"

"What? I can't understand you. Call me back and we'll get a better connection—"

"Penny, it's not the connection. It's me."

"What's the matter?" Her voice dropped its cordiality and became no-nonsense. "Where are you?"

"UCLA Med Center. Look, it's all right. I just bumped into a door—"

"I'm coming out there—"

"Penny, wait a minute. Before you go jumping on a

140

plane, answer me a question. Did you ever remember what it was that—?"

"Well, why do you think I've been trying to get in touch with you?" she answered impatiently. "I remembered what it was and I checked it out so as to have all the information for you—"

"Don't tell me. Let me guess what it is."

"Go ahead, smarty."

"Okay, how's this: two members of Lieutenant Bruno's patrol survived the ambush north of Ban Me Thuot on August seventeenth. They were MEDEVACKED and sent Stateside."

"How'd you know?" She sounded disappointed.

"I was right, huh?"

"Almost. Their names are George Diefenbach—he was a Spec 4 and he teaches high school English at Bowling Green—and Pfc. Gilbert Benoit, who is a gas-station attendant in Albuquerque. Do you want their addresses?"

"No thanks. I've already been in touch with them."

"Do you want to guess anything else?"

"Is there more?"

"A little, and it's kind of grim. You said two survivors, but actually there were three."

"Three?"

"The last man was Private Aaron Hagen—I'm not sure if that's a long *a* or short. He was hit so badly that the support units that pulled out the bodies thought he was dead. They sent him to Graves to be put into a freezer bag and shipped home, but one of the people working there heard him groan and called in the doctors. He lost both arms, both legs, and both eyes, but he's alive. He's the one we did the story on, as a matter of fact. I didn't find out about Diefenbach and Benoit until I checked it out. We never did air the Hagen story," she added with a cynical laugh. "Too strong for television."

"Where can I find him?"

"Veterans Hospital, psychiatric wing, Kiowa City, Iowa."

"Penny?"

"Still here."

"You get on that plane and I'll be waiting."

"We'll see. I thought you were dying or something."

"I'm something. You come on out here and we'll talk about it." I eyed Bunny and found her concentrating on some needlepoint she must have brought with her. Penny and I exchanged a few more clichés and gently disengaged. Without putting down the receiver, I pumped the pegs and asked for another outside line. The operator said I had run up quite a bill. I told her not to worry about it and called the Hall of Records in Atlanta, Georgia. When I said the name, Bunny looked up with a questioning expression.

"What are you calling them for?"

"Never mind why I'm calling them. You just round up my clothes like a good girl. Damn, I wish I had my razor."

"It's here. The police brought over some stuff from your place—"

"That was sweet of them—"

"But you can't expect to walk out of here, Mark. The doctor says—" She stopped in response to a signal from my hand. It was the Atlanta Hall of Records.

"I'm doing an engagement story for the LA *Times*," I informed the clerk, while motioning Bunny to go about collecting my things, "and I'd like to know the birthplace of a Miss Yvonne Page?" I spelled it for him and said it was my understanding that Atlanta was her home town but I wished to make certain for my notice. The clerk asked if I wanted to call back or hold on, as it might take some little time. I elected to hold and did so, while Bunny reluctantly handed me my clothes from the closet (somebody'd had them cleaned) and the clerk rummaged about in his files somewhere near the Atlanta City Hall.

"Yvonne Page." The clerk came back on the line in a nasal drawl. "Born Meechum, Georgia, 1925. That's a suburb of Atlanta," he added. "You might want to point that out to the folks."

"Suburb. Got it. One other thing, just so I don't make any mistakes. This is her first marriage?"

"Why, no. No, it isn't. Miss Page was married once, let me see here . . . where is it? Oh, yes, married once, to Anthony Joseph Bruno. Would you like me to spell it?"

I said it wasn't important.

12 I wasn't in any shape to drive a car, so I gave Bunny the wheel and told her to take me to the airport again. She was confused and upset and whining a lot, feeling that she was somehow compounding a felony by helping me leave a hospital before I was discharged. I assured her that this was not a crime and plugged the cord of my razor into the cigarette lighter unit to save time and keep her quiet. She drove angrily and I didn't entirely blame her. She'd heard one half of two very tantalizing telephone conversations, learning along the way that her brother's fatal patrol had had survivors he'd apparently known nothing about. And she didn't know what importance to attach to this fact. I wasn't sure I did, either. I was playing my last big hunch, based on the old private detective's axiom that when you have eliminated the possible, whatever remains—however improbable—is the truth. I only hoped I'd done the first part.

Finally, I had to turn off the razor. It was killing my face every time it ran over one of my cuts or massaged a bruise. The moment the car was quiet, Bunny started in.

"Mr. Brill"—no more first-naming, I noticed—"will you please tell me where you are going and why?"

"I'm going to Kiowa City to see the queen."

She sighed.

"I don't understand any of this." She stole a sidelong glance at me. "No one's going to talk to you looking like that anyway. You're all yellow and purple-white, except for your eye; it's black. They'll think you've escaped from somewhere."

I said I hoped that wouldn't be so and got out a pencil and my notebook.

"Don't rock the boat," I instructed. "I'm writing stuff down for you to do."

"I'm not doing anything else until you tell me what's going on."

I said nothing until I had finished writing.

"All right, I'll tell you. But it's only what I think, not what I know. Which is why we're avoiding the police for the moment," I explained. "And when they catch up with you, you're to tell them whatever you like— except what I'm telling you now, you understand? This conversation did not take place. Okay?"

"For God's sake."

"All right. In my opinion, your brother was blackmailing Tony Bruno."

"Rollo?" The car swerved in disbelief.

"Watch it. Yes, Rollo."

"But Rollo had plenty of money. He wouldn't need to—and anyway, that's totally unlike him. He wouldn't get mixed up in anything as crummy as that."

"I don't think he was doing it for money. I think he wanted to prevent Tony from running for Congress by threatening to blab something if he went through with it."

"But"—she ran her tongue over her lips as she tried to follow me—"what could he be using? And why? Why would he want to do such a thing? Prevent Tony from going into politics if he felt like it?"

"That I'm not so sure of. At first I thought that he'd found out about Tony's marriage to your stepmother and their continuing relationship after she'd contracted a bigamous marriage with your father, but I don't think he ever knew about that."

She pulled the car off the road.

"What?"

"According to the Atlanta Hall of Records, Yvonne and Tony are married. And I've found at least one witness who'll testify to their meeting once or twice a week on the sly. Get back on the road, Bunny. Planes for Chicago leave on the hour."

"Wait a minute." She rested her head on the steering wheel for some moments, a vein in her right temple throbbing. "Look, that's crazy, about Tony and Yvonne. She must be fifteen years older than he is."

"Stranger things have happened. Come on, drive."

She pulled back onto the freeway.

"I can't believe it."

There was nothing to say so I didn't say it.

"And you think Rollo didn't know about any of this?"

"It's my guess he didn't. He didn't seem to act strange around Yvonne, did he? When she called him over to the house Wednesday night, he went. Besides, if Jacob Fairfield's account is accurate—and I have no reason to suppose it isn't—this whole thing between Tony and Rollo came to a head in prison camp, and although it's possible that Rollo had blurted out to Tony that he knew about his wife, it doesn't exactly fit that Tony would respond with talk about duty and honor. It's possible, but it doesn't sound quite right. And if Rollo *was* keeping Yvonne's adultery under his hat, why was he home for four months without doing anything? As I figure it, he threatened Tony only after he heard Tony was going into politics. After four months at home with Rollo not opening his mouth, Tony must have felt he wasn't going to do anything about it—whatever it was."

"You don't have any ideas?"

"I didn't until Tony got nervous and sent the handicapped after us. Those two were anything but professionals and their impediments and amputations suggested to me that they were veterans. Why would they be in on it? Well, one of them as good as told me that they had something to hide that might come out in my investigation. Maybe Tony's patrol was into dope or something. I'm hoping Private Aaron Hagen is going to tell me."

"I still don't understand how Rollo died."

"Rather cleverly, I think. When Tony got word from Rollo to lay off politics, he called a press conference and gave them a phony-baloney story about Rollo's collaboration activities in prison. Then, when Rollo died, it would look like suicide in the face of disgrace or shame or whatever." I paused and lit a cigarette.

"It's my guess that after your stepmother got through

trying to reason with him in the den that night and went to talk to the cook—or whatever—Bruno wandered in through those open French doors. The conversation continued, but of course there wasn't much he could say because he'd already gone on national television with his charges. Then he pulled out your father's pistol from the desk drawer—he knew it was kept loaded—told Rollo to stand still and blew his head off. Then he squeezed Rollo's hand onto the gun butt and walked out the way he'd come in. If he'd been a little cleverer, he would have remembered Rollo was left-handed and shot him in the other temple and left the gun in his other hand."

"My God. I think I'm going to be sick."

"Don't. You have work to do. When you drop me off, I want you to drive to 9255 Sunset—I've written it down here for you—and go to my lawyer, Tom Honeycutt, on the eighth floor. He looks like a wild man, but don't let that frighten you. You tell him what I've told you and tell him I want him to file a complaint in my behalf for aggravated assault against George Diefenbach of Bowling Green, Ohio, and Gilbert Benoit of Albuquerque. It's all down on this piece of paper."

"Are they the ones who beat you up? Did they kill Margot?"

"It's possible."

"But why?"

"I'm working on it. Now look. The other thing I want you to do—and do it before you leave the airport—" I added, as we pulled into United, "is to call the Kiowa City Veterans Hospital and ask for the chief of the psychiatric wing. Tell him who you are and who I am so

148

he'll be around and co-operate—let's hope—when I get there. You got it?"

"I think so." She pulled to a stop.

"Good girl. And stay with Tom Honeycutt and do what he tells you. Okay?" I opened the car door.

"One more question." She reached over and held my coat sleeve. "Who's Francis?"

"Francis?"

"When you were in the hospital, you talked in your sleep and ran on about someone named Francis. Does he have anything to do with this?"

I hesitated.

"That's Frances with an *e*, Bunny. She was my wife and she was killed in an auto accident on her way to visit her parents in Bakersfield. I dream about her sometimes."

"Oh." She blinked in apologetic surprise. "I'm sorry."

"That's all right." I slammed the door and leaned in the window. "Only you be sure and drive carefully, will you?"

"I promise."

"And stay with Tom. Don't go home. Those guys are still around someplace."

From the way people stared in the airport, I realized I must look pretty bad, even though I'd managed to hide the worst of the damage by pulling my hatbrim down as low as possible. Maybe that only served to increase the unpleasant effect I seemed to be having. I solved the problem by claiming a window seat and looking out of it all the way to Chicago.

I tried to concentrate on the case and what methods

of persuasion I could use to bring Hagen's doctors around, should they prove difficult, but I found my mind straying to thoughts of Frances, and picking up snatches of Penny's conversation in New York. Almost against my will I started fiddling with the puzzle pieces of my own life instead of Rollo's, and wondering if maybe I hadn't simply been so terrified by her death, so scared, that I'd left the force and retreated into a line of work that allowed me to function without really relating to anyone, to do what I had been trained to do without friends or co-workers, to live a kind of emotionally monastic existence devoted to impersonal problem-solving.

It sounded pretty fancy to me, and maybe it was a lot of bullshit; but the ideas kept rattling around and refused to be set aside. Maybe I should consult someone about it. Not an analyst. I didn't have the money for that, and I wasn't entirely sure I believed in them, anyhow.

Maybe Penny would know whom I should see.

No major carrier flies into Kiowa City any more, although Ozark used to. Now in order to get there by air, it was necessary to go to Cedar Rapids, twenty-three miles away, and pick up a shuttle bus. I changed planes at Chicago and got another window to hide my face in. The ground below was a stark contrast to the rolling greenery and desert of Southern California. It looked like an enormous patchwork quilt stretching literally as far as the eye could see. This state is the richest plot of ground in the world. No wonder Khrushchev had gone to take a look.

At Cedar Rapids I got on the bus and rode a bumpy

150

forty minutes into Kiowa City. When I first got off the plane my nostrils were assailed by a strange scent that I decided must be corn, but a fellow passenger who caught me sniffing set me straight.

"Quaker Oats." He pointed, indicating the direction of the town. "That's what you're smelling, bud. Here's where they make Quaker Oats."

I turned to thank him and he backed away without saying good-by. A look at myself in the mirror of the airport's men's room told me why.

Kiowa City on a balmy afternoon in late June looked like a damn pleasant place to live. The campus and the town seemed inextricably intertwined and a good many enormous green elms responding to the sun gave the place an almost tropical cast. The bus let me off at a corner parking-lot depot that sat behind an aged hotel. I walked through the lobby and came out on a street that bordered the university campus. In front of the hotel was a hack stand. I got into a cab and told the driver to take me to the Veterans Hospital. He kept a piece of straw in his mouth and his portable radio turned on as we turned into traffic.

The station to which he was listening evidently belonged to the university. Either that, or the farmers around here got a big charge out of *Philoctetes*, which was what we were hearing. Maybe both.

"That's a pretty fancy radio station you got there." I leaned forward.

"Oldest station west of the Mississip," he commented, and didn't elaborate.

We went down a big hill (I always had imagined this state flat as a pancake, but apparently it was not true of the eastern portion), and crossed a dirty-looking river that was straddled by a number of attractive footbridges.

"That's the Kiowa." The driver gestured, reading my mind.

Veterans Hospital was a huge red-brick structure about a mile away from University Hospital ("one of the finest in the country," according to my informant) and far less attractive.

Veterans' hospitals are about the most depressing places you can find and this one was no exception. The main lobby was dark and gloomy, although it rested your eyes from the glare outside. There were no groups of families waiting to visit their relatives, only one or two unhappy-looking people sitting by themselves and nervously glancing at their watches. I pictured them torn between duty, love, and horror. They were afraid to come here and afraid not to. The patients probably felt the same way; desperate for love, for contact, and at the same time embarrassed, ashamed, and in some cases not even knowing that they'd had it. Is there any point in visiting a vegetable?

The veterans' hospitals had begun thinning out in the years after World War II and Korea. Now Vietnam had come to fill them up again with a new store of human debris.

I walked up to the information desk and the nurse there blenched at the sight of me. Visitors weren't supposed to look bad.

"I'm here to see the head of the psychiatric wing," I told her. "My name is Brill and I believe I'm expected."

"Mr. Brill," she repeated uncertainly. "Just a minute, please." She picked up her telephone and punched a couple of buttons in the front of it. "Dr. Arnheim, I have a Mr. Brill in the lobby." She sounded almost timid. "He says—yes—yes, doctor. I'll tell him." She hung up and looked nervously up to me. "Will you have a seat? The doctor's on his way."

"Thank you."

I didn't have long to wait. Arnheim came walking out of an elevator that opened at the end of a long corridor leading off from the lobby. He was tall and remarkably handsome. If he hadn't been taking care of soldiers who'd had their brains scrambled, he might have won a Hollywood film contract. Movie producers believed that eyes as blue as his were worth millions, and with his teeth and jawbone thrown in, they couldn't have missed. He strode rapidly into the lobby, looked around for a second, and pegged me as his visitor.

"Mr. Brill?"

I stood up and shook hands.

"What's this all about? You look as though you'd been in a fight," he commented in a tone of concern as we started walking back down the corridor.

"I have been. Can we go to your office? I'll try to explain why I'm here."

He said we could, and we did. There he sat and listened attentively from behind his desk, while I asked him if he'd heard about Sergeant Rollins' death, and generally amplified on what Bunny had told him over the phone.

"There's a strong possibility Harold Rollins was murdered," I concluded, "and it's my hunch he was killed to prevent his disclosing something that happened on that patrol. Two survivors of that patrol roughed me up a bit and as good as told me they didn't want me looking into it. At the time I didn't see how I could. Then I heard about Private Hagen, and here I am, hoping he can help me out."

"They didn't kill you," Arnheim pointed out. "Surely that would have been a permanent solution to their worries. And if they killed one person, why not in for a penny, in for a pound?"

"There are a few possibilities," I replied, unwilling to go into it with him. "They may have thought they left me for dead, or perhaps they are not the killers I'm looking for. Also, I'm a former cop, with connections. I'm hoping Private Hagen can set me straight."

"What if he can't?" the doctor asked, without expression.

I got up and started walking around the cramped office.

"I'm not sure. Look, doctor, I'm not asking you to put Private Hagen on any witness stands." I thought I saw him smile. "All I want to do is ask him some questions. If he tells me what I want to know—if he even comes near it—then I think I can go ahead and pursue this case without ever dragging him any further into it than this interview. He can talk, can't he?"

"Oh, he can speak, if that's what you mean. His mouth and vocal cords are about the only part of him that's intact."

"Then what's to prevent my seeing him? Just for fifteen minutes?"

"Well, the main thing is he's dead."

"Come again?"

"He thinks he's dead." Arnheim put his hands to-gether on his desk and made a church steeple with the tips of his fingers. "It's hard to dispute his logic when you think about it. He was found and mistaken for dead, sent to Graves to be washed down and put into storage, woke up and found himself surrounded by corpses. He hasn't got any legs, arms, or eyes. Everything has to be done for him—feeding, helping him defecate, blowing his nose. He thinks this is heaven and has the idea that the nurses are angels. That view isn't hard to dispute, either," he added.

"But you say he talks."

"Oh, yes."

"Does he seem sane, aside from this delusion?"

Arnheim sighed, pulled out a pipe, and began to fill it from a humidor on his desk.

"That's a mighty big 'aside' you're talking about. He appears to make sense on a great many subjects, but I must emphasize the word 'appears.' "

"Has he ever mentioned the patrol?"

Arnheim puffed on his pipe in troubled silence for some moments.

"When he first came here, almost four years ago, he talked about a great many things. It was very hard to separate the fact from the fancy."

"Are you trying to tell me that some things he raved about that you thought were delusions may in fact have occurred? What was he saying back then?"

"I'd rather you heard that from Hagen himself—if he'll go into it with you."

"Then you'll let me see him?"

"On certain conditions, all right, I will. And let's make no mistake about what the conditions are," he continued, sternly. "First and most important: if he shows any sign of becoming upset with your questions, out you go and that's the end of it. And I will not tell you anything he may have told me. Second: you are not to attribute anything you learn here to Hagen in any court of law." He pointed the stem of his pipe in my direction by way of interrupting my protests. "That's absolute, Mr. Brill. Aaron Hagen has gone through all the tortures of the damned, and he's going to continue going through them here for the rest of his life. His physical condition is irreparable and I don't think the chances are much better for his mental state, but I am not going to expose him to anything that may undo what little progress we've made. I wouldn't even consider letting you do what you're asking if the matter of Sergeant Rollins' death weren't of such obvious moment. Now, will you agree to my conditions?"

"All right. But how do you know you can trust me?" I couldn't resist asking. He smiled.

"You have an honest face, what's left of it." He stood up. "Shall we go? He's generally up from his nap at about this time."

"Will it bother him—my face, I mean?"

"I don't think so," he reminded me, holding open the door.

13 "There's just one thing," Arnheim said, as we entered the elevator. "You must remember that he thinks this is heaven." He smiled with sad irony. "And you have to play along with that part of it. I'll introduce you as the Archangel Gabriel," he decided. "I don't think we've had an Archangel Gabriel before, and you'll have to ad-lib any references he may make. Can you do that?"

"I think so."

"This way. Don't look left or right if it bothers you."

He led me down another long corridor, this one painted a cheery white, past open doors and open wards in which sat or slept the terrible by-products of war, those unseen catastrophes that society tucks away from sight before the treaties have been signed and the ground changes hands. Everything was white—the walls, the sheets, the furniture, the bandages. And quiet. Was it so quiet because of the lazy summer afternoon's heat? Or because strangers were present? My footsteps echoed sacrilegiously on the white linoleum. Arnheim wore rubber soles. This section housed the double-damned, I thought; not only had they no bodies, but their minds had been shattered as well. Or maybe they were better off. Maybe this final retreat was easier to bear than the rational comprehension of what they had become. If being cared for hand and foot (an awkward phrase) meant you were in heaven, perhaps that was a more practical way of looking at it. (Another unfortunate choice of words.)

"Does anyone come to visit him?" I found myself speaking in a whisper, although we were probably too far from anyone to be overheard.

"His father, sometimes. He lives in the Amana colonies not far from here. Of course he has to play dead in order to talk to his son and that upsets him, so he doesn't stop by too often." Two nurses in starched white uniforms strode silently past and flicked a smile at Arnheim.

I thought I could hear a choir singing somewhere ahead of me—a section from Handel's *Messiah:* "For Unto Us a Child Is Born."

"He's listening to the cassette," Arnheim explained, as we drew nearer. "Only sacred music, of course. His ideas of heaven are extremely well defined. He's had a lot of time to work them out," he noted sourly. "Oh, and one other thing. You'll find he shares his room with another soldier, but don't worry about it."

"Won't we disturb him?"

"It's not likely. He was shelled for so long one night in 1968 that he can't hear any more. Here we are." He stopped at a closed door, behind which I could hear the

158

choir. "You'll have to let it keep playing." Arnheim put a finger to his lips. "Are you ready?"

I nodded, the sweat running down from my armpits and trickling its way to my groin. I hoped I wasn't going to be sick. I eyed Arnheim's perfect profile as he slowly opened the door. Life is more ridiculous than you can imagine.

"Aaron?" We were inside the room and standing at the foot of a bed. At the head of the bed a figure appeared to be sitting up. Actually, he was standing. Below him, where his legs should have been, the white linen was tucked in crisply and neatly. The figure at the head of the bed had a forehead strangely bent and scarred, empty eye sockets. He wore a white shirt that had been made with no holes for arms. Next to him, on another bed, a body lay underneath a single sheet, the head turned away from my view. Throughout my visit, it never made a move.

"Hello, Saint Peter." Hagen's voice was surprisingly strong and resonant. If you talked to him on the telephone or heard him on the radio you'd never know. "What brings you here?" Tucked next to Hagen's torso was plastic tubing that entered his body at various points beneath his shirt.

"I've brought somebody to see you," Arnheim said gently.

Quietly he went to the table between the beds and picked up a pair of sunglasses, which he deftly slipped over Hagen's terrible eyes.

"Really? Who?"

"The Archangel Gabriel would like to ask you some questions."

"The Archangel? No shit. How are you, Gabe?"

"Just fine, Aaron. How are you?"

"Fine and dandy. Hard to be anything but, up here. How's the trumpet?"

"I'm keeping a stiff upper lip." I looked at the doctor for approval but he kept his eyes on Hagen.

"Hey, that's a riot, Gabe. That was really funny." He had a hearty, robust laugh. "Boy that was funny." His laughter subsided and turned into a cough. Arnheim held him tenderly and patted him until it ceased. As our conversation continued, he picked up the chart at the end of the bed and examined it.

"Well, what'd you want to ask me about?" Hagen faced in the direction of my voice.

"It's about the patrol, Aaron."

"Patrol?" His voice took on a frown.

"You know, back on earth?"

"Oh, the *patrol*." He was chipper again. "I didn't know what you meant for a minute there. It's been so long. Hell, Gabe, what do you want to know about that for? It was a bummer. Sorry," he amended with a smile. "I know I'm not supposed to say hell around here, but it's hard to change the habits of a lifetime."

"That's all right. The thing is, Aaron, I'm making a report about what happened on the patrol—"

"A report?" He sounded suspicious.

"That's right." I tried to chuckle. "There's a lot of paper work up here, you know. Would you care to talk to me about it?"

"Well . . ." He stretched the word unwillingly. Arnheim looked up from the chart and watched him closely. If he said no, the whole trip would be for nothing. "If

160

you really want to hear about it I'll tell you," Hagen decided. "But I'm telling you, Gabe, it was a bummer."

"I know it was, Aaron. We're just trying to update our records."

"Did you talk to any of the other guys?"

"Did I—?"

"They're in a different section. You know that, Aaron." Arnheim came to my rescue. "Gabe is going to get to them. He just thought he'd start with you."

"I'd like to know what section the lieutenant's in." Hagen's voice turned hard. "Did you guys let him in here? That's the limit." His lip started to tremble.

"He's not up here," I said quickly. "We didn't admit him. That's part of what we want to get an update on."

"If you let him in you'll be sorry." Hagen appeared somewhat mollified by my response. "You'll be sorry, that's all I can tell you."

"What happened?"

"It was supposed to be a sweep. Day and a half, maybe two. The lieutenant took two squads out and then we divided. I went with the lieutenant and Sergeant Kissick went with the other squad. We were going to make a big circle and we had a fixed point for rendezvous at 1800."

"Sergeant Rollins was with you?"

"That's right. He carried the radio. Then there was Baker, Fox, Diefenbach, Colma, Benoit, Mayer, Lewin, and me. Oh, and Grubowski."

"Where did you go?"

"Gee, I can't tell you that, Gabe. I really don't know. We were some fifteen miles northwest of Ban Me Thuot

161

when we left the fire base. We may even have crossed over into Cambodia, but I don't think so."

"Go on." According to recent Pentagon revelations that's just where they could have been.

"Well, we came into this little ville and that's where it happened."

"Tell me about it." The saliva in my mouth had disappeared suddenly.

He sighed.

"Well, it's kind of hard. It all happened so fast, when it happened."

"You don't have to tell Gabriel if you don't want to," Arnheim said softly.

"Well, it doesn't thrill me, I can tell you that. But if it's really important—"

"It is," I said.

"Then I guess I can make it. Let me see. Diefenbach and Colma were up ahead cutting point, and they got in there first, and then we followed. It was just a little clearing in the jungle, you know. Nothing big. Only twenty huts at most, I'd say. And there weren't any men about, almost none that I could see, except for a couple of old geezers and some kids whose nuts probably hadn't dropped yet. Sorry."

"Go on."

"Well, the lieutenant—"

"Lieutenant Bruno?"

"That's right. He came in and took charge. He seemed kinda spooked to find the ville. I guess it wasn't on any of his maps. We went in real cautiouslike, because we didn't know—maybe the place was honeycombed with NVA. You following me, Gabe?"

162

"I'm right with you."

"It was kinda scary, I admit, because they all sat and looked at us, and some wouldn't come out of their huts. I guess they were just as scared as we were. But we couldn't tell if they were scared or unfriendly, you know? And then that woman came running toward us—"

"What woman?"

"I don't know. Just some young woman who was there. She was holding a white rag and running down the center of the ville and waving this rag—and she was carrying something in her other fist." He swallowed. "The lieutenant yelled out that it was a grenade, and called for us to open fire. We were so jumpy, we did. We blasted her head off and then there was screaming and some babies began to cry, and then—I don't know —then it started to happen. The lieutenant was screaming that the ville was full of Charley and we started shooting everything that moved and setting fire to the huts. I don't know how long it took us but we mowed down that entire ville. Everybody sort of went off his head there for a while, I guess. We were damn near shooting each other we were so hot. And then Sergeant Rollins started screaming to stop, and the lieutenant hit him across the mouth and told him to shut up. By this time all there was was a pile of smoking huts and bodies. More bodies than you'd ever—and you know what? We hadn't killed a single male of combat age or capability. Not one, out of eighty and some odd women and kids and old men." He stopped.

"Are you all right?"

"Me? Yeah, I'm fine. It's just that I don't like to

remember that part too much. You can understand why. I practically didn't make it up here on account of that." He was silent again and I sat on the edge of the bed, because my legs wouldn't hold me up, and listened to the music. An alto was singing:

Then shall the eyes of the blind be opened, and the ears of the dead unstopped. Then shall the lame man leap as an hart, and the tongue of the dumb shall sing. He shall feed his flock like a shepherd, and He shall gather the lambs with His arm, and carry them in His bosom, and gently lead those that are young.

I looked at Arnheim. He was staring at his chart with unseeing eyes, as though Hagen's statement or the singer had rooted him to the spot.

"What did you do then?"

"We dug a trench, five standing guard while the others worked." Hagen spoke quietly, sadly. "The lieutenant ordered us to shove the bodies in the trench. And we did. Then we covered it all over. Then the lieutenant gathered us all around and said that our target practice had got a little out of hand. That was what he called it," Hagen remembered. "Target practice. He made it seem as though we'd all gone berserk, but not really him. He said in order to protect ourselves from the consequences of our getting out of hand, it would be a good idea if we all agreed not to talk about it to anyone when we got back to the fire base. Or after. He said there was no doubt in his mind that this ville belonged to Charley and that what proved it was that that woman

164

with the white rag had been carrying a grenade to us. Which was true, only when we looked at the grenade we found she hadn't even pulled the pin. She'd been coming to give it to us, was how I saw it. Charley'd probably been there and left it behind and she was trying to give it to us. But we were all too scared and shook to argue, so we all agreed with the lieutenant and swore to keep our mouths shut.

"Then we started off toward the rendezvous and got ambushed by Charley. They must have been near the ville watching the whole thing. They waited until after the flankers and the point cutters had gone all the way past where they were hidden and then they opened up from all around us. Sergeant Rollins got on the radio right away to try and let somebody know our position and to ask for support before we were wiped out, and the rest of us did our best to return the fire." He sighed. "That's where we all were killed. Is there anything else you want to know?"

"Did you ever learn the name of the ville you wiped out?"

"The lieutenant couldn't find it on his map. He said he thought it might be a place called An Lo, but he wasn't sure."

"An Lo?"

"I think so." I looked over at Arnheim, who pointed to the dial on his wristwatch. I nodded.

"Well, Aaron, that appears to take care of everything—"

"Uh—Gabe. You mind if I ask you a question?"

"Go right ahead. I'll answer it if I can."

The blind torso seemed to shift its position slightly.

*I know that my Redeemer liveth, and that
He shall stand at the latter day upon the
earth. And though worms shall destroy this
body, yet in my flesh shall I see God.*

"Those people we killed, those women and their
children. Did they make it?"

"Make it?" I looked over at Arnheim again and saw
him pointing with his index finger toward the ceiling.
"Up here, you mean?" Hagen nodded, rapidly. "Yes,
Aaron, they made it. Every last one."

"Thank good Christ."

"Amen, Aaron. I'm going now."

"Come again sometime, Gabe."

"I'll try, but of course I can't promise."

"I understand. So long."

"So long, Aaron." Arnheim laid a hand on his shoulder of stubble. "I'll be talking to you later, okay?"

"Okay." The rich trembling tones of a baritone followed us out of the room.

*Why do the nations so furiously rage to-
gether? And why do the people imagine a
vain thing?*

"Well, did you get what you want?" Arnheim asked,
as we stood waiting for the elevator doors to open.
"Where are you off to now?"

"San Jose."

Even in the elevator I heard it, or thought I did.

*Hallelujah! for the Lord God Omnipotent
reigneth. The kingdom of this world is be-*

come the kingdom of our Lord, and of His
Christ; and he shall reign for ever and
ever. King of Kings, and Lord of Lords,
Hallelujah!

Up until now it had always made me think of Christmas.

14 It was midnight exactly when I touched down at the San Jose Municipal Airport. Planes from Chicago to San Jose don't leave all the time, so I'd had to spend a few hours at O'Hare, biting my nails and hoping that nobody was going to bolt. I still couldn't call the police, because the only proof I was hoping to get would come from surprising a confession, and I was the only person in a position to do that.

I called San Jose from Chicago and asked information for an Anthony Bruno for Congress headquarters and they obliged me with a listing less than three days old. I called the number and a pert voice answered, "Volunteers for Bruno. Good afternoon."

I explained that I was from the New York *Times* and was on my way to San Jose to do a story on Anthony Bruno and where would I find him this evening, did she know? She became understandably excited—no politician can do better than the New York *Times*—and paused to check the Major's schedule. She referred to him as "the Major," but sometimes she called him "Tony."

"He's going to be addressing the Rotarians this evening at a dinner at the Ramada Inn, across from the Civic Center. It'll be in the Comingore Room, beginning at eight."

"The Commodore Room?"

She spelled it for me and said she hoped I could make it.

By the time I got there, it was almost over. The Rotarians were working on their coffee and dessert, and Major Anthony J. Bruno, clearly the guest of honor for the occasion, was standing, in full uniform and chest covered with medals, behind a portable rostrum with microphone. It had been set up at the center of the VIP table, a straight-on creation with white tablecloth, at which were seated all the bigwigs and their wives looking strangely reminiscent of the *Last Supper*. For Tony Bruno, in a way it was.

I stood at the back of the room in the dark next to a red-coated waiter who was leaning up against the doorframe, and we both listened to Bruno's concluding words. He stook straight and tall and manly, his hair cropped short, his eyes unblinkingly front, firm of jaw and of purpose.

"I want to conclude by thanking you all for coming here tonight and hearing what I have to say. In a few days I'll put aside this wonderful uniform—forever, in all likelihood—and then I'll be in a position to amplify my views further and in greater detail. But I don't think I'm stepping out of line when I say that recent events have shown that politics and politicians have gone to the dogs and I think it's time we did something about that. I thank you."

Bruno's words were received with enthusiastic applause, which culminated in a haphazard standing ovation of the type that may be expected when your audience has just put away a four- or five-course dinner and been sitting on its butt for three hours.

As the applause continued, I took out my notebook, scribbled two words on a page, tore it out, and handed it to the waiter.

"Give this to the Major for me, will you?"

"Sure thing." He took the paper and threaded his way through the tables toward the dais, where Bruno was receiving handshakes he had to lean down to acknowledge and the president was trying to call the meeting to order in order to adjourn it properly.

I watched the waiter's red coat as he wormed his way through the little knot of well-wishers and passed my message up to the guest of honor. Bruno gave him a brief nod of thanks, opened the paper, and abruptly sat down. By then the president had restored order and turned to thank the guest of honor for his enlightening and stimulating discussion of the issues. He ended with a pointed hope we'd all hear more of him in the near future, when, as he had said, he would be able to speak with greater candor. Now was there a motion to adjourn? There was, and people began drifting out.

Bruno continued to sit in his chair, holding the piece of notebook page between his hands and staring dumbly down at it. I leaned up against the door in the shadows at the entrance to the large room and watched him. People continued to walk up and wish him well, and someone asked if he could offer him a lift—at least that's what it looked like he was offering—but Bruno's head came up with a jerk and a wan smile and shook a no-thank-you. He continued to respond as in a dream to the departing Rotarians, but I could tell the sound had been turned off in his mind and he was just going through the motions. Someone wanted his autograph.

The Rotarians were tired and didn't take too long to get the lead out. Most of them would have to be at work in the morning and it was after twelve. It's amazing how fast a roomful of maybe three hundred people can empty when the exits are clearly marked, the doors open out, and they want to get home.

In just about five minutes there were only two people in the Comingore Room. Slowly, Tony Bruno lifted his head up from my note and peered out into the darkness with a squint. I stepped into the light a little way to help him.

"Major Bruno? My name is Brill. Can we talk?"

He leaned over and squinted at me some more.

"What about?" He took yet another look. "You look like you ought to see a doctor."

"I've seen several. About An Lo."

"An what? I'm afraid I don't know what you're talking about." But his forehead knew; it had suddenly become very shiny, and Bruno himself seemed frozen in a half-up half-down position in his chair, leaning over the table as though he had suddenly been cast in bronze at an awkward moment.

"An Lo. And if you don't know what I'm talking about, perhaps you'll know what George Diefenbach and Gilbert Benoit are talking to the LA police and district attorney about. I understand there's an inspector general on his way out from Washington this evening."

"That's a lie!" Bruno thundered, still unable to move, although his voice was shattering. Someone hadn't yet turned off the public-address system. And he was still pinpointed by a spotlight.

"No it's not," I lied. "The party's over, Major. Your target practice has got a little out of hand."

His face went white and staring, his body slid back into his chair.

"I don't understand." He meant it as a whisper but it went right into the microphone.

"What don't you understand? That you got caught? That Diefenbach and Benoit couldn't go through with it when the pressure was on? You should be ashamed of yourself, hiring those two shell-shocked boys to do your dirty work for you. It may pay to hire the vet, Major, but you've got to give him work he can do."

"They had just as much to lose as I," Bruno mused hoarsely, trying to figure it out. Either he had never learned about Aaron Hagen, or had never anticipated his telling a coherent story. I suspected the former. Hagen had been officially labeled dead. By the time he was discovered, Bruno was off in POW camp.

"As much to lose as you?" I walked through the deserted tables toward him. "I don't think so, do you? Really? One of them pumping gas and the other teaching school? You were on your way to Congress. That was something Rollo just couldn't sit back and watch you do, wasn't it?"

"Listen, Brill." He got up and came around the end of the table and down to me, standing very close and breathing heavily into my face. "What'll you take?" He brushed away my expression with a brusque gesture. "Aw, come on. Come on! A bunch of gooks on the other side of the world! Commies! That gook broad was coming at me with a grenade—"

"With the pin still in it—"

"She had her finger in the goddamn ring!" he insisted, grabbing me by the shoulders and shaking them. "Anyway, what's the difference? It all happened so long ago. Five years! For Christ's sake, Brill, it's all over and done with. Nobody gives a damn. Now what do you want? Money? You want money? You can have it. You wanna join my staff? Name your salary—"

"I thought you were going to clean up politics," I reminded him.

"Brill, cut the crap! This is serious!"

"I think so, too. But it isn't just a matter of An Lo. Maybe you're right, I don't know. I wasn't there. Maybe it was riddled with Charley—"

"It was, it was!" He was shaking my shoulders again.

"But what about Rollo? And Margot Koontz? You and your wife have got to explain all about that, and I—"

"My *what?*" He stopped, dead still, his hands frozen on my shoulders, not for emphasis but for support. The man was drowning in the middle of a convention hall with not enough left over in the glasses nearby to swim in.

"Let's not be coy, Major." This conversation was beginning to tire me. "You know who I'm talking about. Diefenbach and Benoit weren't up for killing me and they weren't up for killing anybody else, either. And you've been up here all the time."

"My *wife?*" He looked at me, eyeball to eyeball, the sweat streaming down his cheeks and nose, his eyes unblinking, and slowly going mad, two inches from me.

Then he started to laugh. It was just a chuckle at first, a kind of snigger. Then it got bigger and bigger until he could hardly breathe, and tears joined the drops of perspiration on his face. His laughter became uncontrollable and bent him double—his hands still clutching my shoulders in a viselike grip.

"My wife!" he bellowed, and went on laughing until he was choking with it, heaving and wheezing with hilarity.

I looked into his bulging catlike green eyes and finally understood.

Past the quaking insignia on his shoulder, I could see the waiters coming in to clean up.

_15_ I knew someone was in my apartment without opening the door because I could hear them moving inside. I went back down to my car, unlocked the glove compartment, and returned with my gun before putting the key in the door. It was dark inside—which wasn't unusual since it was after three in the morning—but someone was there all right. A cigarette end glowed in the black.

"Who's there?" Bunny's voice trembled as I switched on the light. "Oh, Mark, for heaven's sake." She stubbed out the cigarette and got quickly to her feet. She'd been stretched out on the couch.

"What are you doing here, Bunny?"

"I could ask you the same question. Are you going to keep waving that thing around?" She gestured in the direction of the gun. "Your friend Tom Honeycutt brought me here for the night. He's in your room, asleep. He offered to take the couch, but I told him I couldn't sleep anyway." She shrugged.

"Well, we'll try not to wake him." I put the safety back on and stuffed the gun into my pocket.

"What did you learn? Have you been in Kiowa City all this time?" She sat down again and patted the seat next to her.

"I made a stop or two on my way back." I stalled, looking her in the eyes while I took off my jacket and made a big deal out of hanging it up.

"Well, what's the story?"

"Let me ask you two questions first. Where was your mother Monday afternoon?"

"Monday?" She bit her thumb. "She went out to Brentwood on some errands. I stayed home—as you directed. When she came in the house the phone was ringing. You know the rest. Can I turn this out again? It hurts my eyes. What's your other question?"

"It's about Clarisse. She's been with your family a long time, hasn't she?"

"Clarisse, oh my yes. She was with Yvonne before she met Father. What's she got to do with it?"

"Not much, but in a way, a lot. Let me fill you in."

So I filled her in. It wasn't easy, and much of it sounded lunatic to my ears as I told it. But I reflected that it *was* lunatic and plowed ahead. Bunny sat in the dark and listened as though turned to stone—a human being petrifying with every word I spoke. When it was over, I asked if she was all right. It took her a while to move, and when she did, it was to sag against my chest. She started to cry the way babies do—with no sound at first, like a film that's out of sync with the dialogue. I held her for a while, saying nothing, because there wasn't anything I could say, and remembered a similar

176

scene we'd played together on a late-night jet flight that seemed ages ago. Then I'd had a lot to say; then Bunny's problems had been merely terrible. Now they were grotesque.

Not knowing what to do, I continued to hold her in my arms and I kissed her several times on top of her head. She was wearing the same perfume she'd had on the day we met. We might have been back on the plane.

It was a while before I realized she was responding to my kisses with some of her own. They were becoming fierce and ardent in the tear-stained dark.

"Bunny—"

"Mark, I love you—"

"Bunny—"

"Please, *please!* Don't say anything, just—"

"Bunny, listen to me. I've got to say something." With an effort both physical and emotional, I gripped her by the shoulders and pushed her away.

"I don't want to hear it. I just—why can't we just—"

"Because you don't love me—"

"I do," she protested, a wail in her voice as she leaned toward me again.

"You don't. You just think you do."

"I defy you to tell me the difference. And don't patronize me. Even if you're right, that's no reason to go around throwing beautiful women away. Someday there may be a shortage. Or can't you stand touching a member of my charming family?"

"You know that isn't so. Can I turn on the light?"

"Suit yourself."

She'd lit another cigarette by the time I found the switch.

"Look, I don't mean to patronize you. You're a very attractive girl and—"

"Never mind. The moment has passed." She wouldn't look at me. I sighed, got up, and took down my jacket.

"I've got to get going now anyway," I said.

She didn't appear to have heard me.

"It's that woman you talked to in New York, isn't it?"

"Yes. Bunny, I'm going now."

"Now?" She blinked. "But it's only—"

"It's got to be now. Will you be here when I get back?"

"I guess." She shrugged and came around to face me by the door. "I'm sorry if I made a fool of myself just now. You caught me off guard with your news."

"You didn't make a fool of yourself. I'll probably be kicking myself an hour from now."

"You're a regular little gentleman." She occupied herself with fixing my tie.

"You'll stay here?"

She looked up at me. Her face was bleary but her eyes weren't.

"If you say so. Mark—" I stopped, my hand on the knob. "You'll do it—" She fumbled for the word and sniffed. "You'll do it gently, won't you?"

"As gently as I can."

She nodded rapidly several times in succession. "I'm turning this out again," she said, before I'd closed the door.

I couldn't ever remember being so tired. And I didn't want to think about why I was. I just wanted this next part to be over and done with. I was feeling things; pieces of machinery in my soul that I thought had rusted—pieces I'd faked in my relationships with peo-

178

ple for the past ten years—had begun achingly to grind and groan to life. It made you tire faster when they were working. Perhaps that was why so many folks preferred to do without them.

The house looked the way it did when I first laid eyes on it. Vast. Still. Peaceful, yet strangely disturbed in the predawn hour. Maybe it was the drawn shades that played tricks with its appearance. As I got out of my car I heard a couple of jays carrying on an animated discussion in the stillness on the lawn.

I rang the bell, expecting the butler or Clarisse to put in a sleepy appearance after a few minutes, but I was wrong; she opened the door herself.

Yvonne Rollins looked older in the morning light, or maybe other things had combined to age her suddenly. Her skin was drawn more tightly over her cheeks and the ridges in her throat were suddenly pronounced. But she was fully dressed and compensating for reality with a great deal of make-up. When she saw me, her eyes clouded over for a moment.

"You look a sight," she commented dully. "Come in." Her breath almost hung in the morning air. She'd been drinking. She turned and went back into the house, leaving the door open for me to follow. She didn't look back, but glided like a sleepwalker into the den. I closed both doors behind us and we sat down across from each other in the dim light. Her face was hidden in the recesses of the room.

"What was it you wanted to see me about?" Her voice had a toneless quality, as though calling on people at this hour without notice was not a remarkable occurrence.

"I've just come from San Jose." I found I wasn't certain just where to begin.

"You made good time." She wasn't going to help me.

"I came by private charter. How are you feeling, Mrs. Rollins?"

"Not too well." She accepted the change of subject without comment. "Dr. Carstairs gave me some pills but they don't seem to help. I haven't been getting any sleep."

"Have you heard from Tony?"

"They allowed him one phone call."

"Would you care to tell me about Rollo now?"

Her shoulders hunched imperceptibly, then slackened.

"What is there to tell?"

"You called him over here to talk about Major Bruno's charges last Wednesday evening."

"Yes."

"What happened?"

"I shot him." Her frail voice had a trace of impatience in it. "It was the last thing in the world he expected. He was standing over there"—she indicated the spot, to which the Indian rug had now been returned, with a slight jerk of her head—"and I went up to him and put the gun to his head and pulled the trigger. Just like that. It wasn't hard," she added.

"To prevent his telling people about An Lo?"

"That was a vicious, depraved lie!" She sparked to life. "A damnable lie. Rollo always hated Tony. Tony was everything Rollo wanted to be and couldn't. He knew the General always preferred Tony to him and wished Tony was his own child. That's why he made up that dreadful story. If Tony hadn't thought up a way to

180

keep Rollo quiet, he would have ruined his entire life. Can you imagine a person so filled with hate that he would do a thing like that? Can you?"

"Why did your cook provide you with an alibi for the shooting, Mrs. Rollins?"

"Clarisse?" There was a faint smile in her voice. "That's rather a long story."

I decided to let her save it for later.

"What about Margot Koontz? She called you, I take it?"

"She'd been going through some of Rollo's things, cleaning up and such, and had stumbled across a type-written signed statement Rollo had left in her desk when he had used it to write up his dirty piece of blackmail. It was a carbon of the one he'd mailed Tony, telling him he was going to tell the truth, as he put it, about—about that place. She wanted to know what to do. I told her I'd come over and we'd talk about it. I told Bunny I was going to run some errands. I drove to Woodland Hills. When she let me in and showed me the letter, I shot her. That wasn't hard, either." She gave a gentle sigh. "I didn't use the same gun, of course. I'm not dumb. The General has a lot of weapons stored in the attic. I wouldn't let him display too many of them. It isn't genteel. Then I came home. Just in time for the police to tell me about it."

"Can we talk about your son for a minute?"

There was a tic of silence.

"I've told you everything I know. I wiped off my prints and squeezed his fingers around the handle on the floor. The coroner's inquest couldn't fault it. Poor Rollo. I did try to be a good mother to him, you know."

"Not your stepson, Mrs. Rollins. Your son."

A ray of morning light streamed in through the window beneath the bottom of the shade and caught her in its beam. Her face sagged and seemed to fragment, all the features suddenly coming apart from each other and going off in different directions. Only her heavy make-up contrived to hold it together.

"I spoke to the bartender at the Dixie Cup," I said quietly, trying to keep my promise to Bunny but finding it harder by the minute. "I imagine there are motels in the vicinity that would recognize your pictures."

She sat still for some moments more, her face being torn apart by the light, but she didn't seem to notice or blink her eyes.

"You think you understand everything," she said finally, a smile tugging at the corners of her mouth and her Southern accent becoming playfully more pronounced. "You're so clever, Mr. Brill. And so persistent."

"I'm sure you could tell me things I don't know."

"I'll wager I could at that." She thought about it for a long time, almost fondly, it seemed, across the room from me.

"I could tell you about a fifteen-year-old girl in the Georgia boondocks who found out she was going to have a baby and ran away from home to the big city. I could tell you how she passed herself off as eighteen and married a sergeant at Fort Benning named Tony Bruno, a frightened but gentle young man from the wilds of Brooklyn. I could tell you how the frightened but gentle young husband went off to fight and how the girl waited for him. And how he died on Omaha Beach and left her with nothing but his name and a few dollars. And her baby.

"Maybe I could even tell you how the girl took the baby with her to New Orleans and found a job that suited her looks, her poverty, and her education. I could tell you about life in one of the fanciest whorehouses in New Orleans." She addressed me directly. "And tell you more about Louisiana politics than you'd ever find out in books. Because I—that girl, she stayed in that whorehouse for years and years, saving her money, and never, *never* giving up that baby boy. Even though it meant spending some of her hard-earned money on a poor, starving Creole girl from off the streets to help her look after him."

"Clarisse Marengo?"

"Well, don't sound so surprised, Mr. Brill. You're just getting the stuff of which Grand Guignol is made. It has to come from somewhere, you know."

As she spoke, her cultivated accent, like her artificial face, was slowly dissolving. Her Southern drawl was getting broader by the minute.

"That part isn't too hard to grasp, now is it? For a clever and persistent man like yourself?" I could swear she batted her eyelashes in my direction.

"But could I tell you what happened between that girl and her son?" She went on in a more reflective vein before I had time to answer. "Could I explain to you the friendship, the deep and abiding love that grew between her and the only person in the world she really trusted, and who returned that love and trust? I don't think so. You want to know something?" She turned and faced me, the smile more pronounced and more ludicrous.

"He was the only man who ever satisfied me. That's right, Mr. Brill. My son. My son was the only man who ever did. And I'm the only girl he's ever loved. What do you think of that? Well, of course it's disgustin'," she replied for me, playing another part with shocked Southern propriety. "Yes, I thought it was pretty awful, too. I even tried to see a doctor about it, what do you think of that? I tried." She sat back and sighed as though she were played out. "Yes, I could tell you all that, but would you understand it? I doubt it. You're clever, Mr. Brill, but I doubt you're understandin'. It's probably much easier for the likes of you to simply sit back and be appalled."

"I'm just listening to your story, Mrs. Rollins," I lied. In any case, she didn't appear to have heard me.

"Then, of course, the girl and the boy and the maid left New Orleans with their savings and came out to California and started fresh. And did they study, and read, and work hard so they could join the civilized world? Well, you just bet they did—all of them. And that boy went off to college and he got straight A's, let me tell you. And then he came home and told his mother about his fine upright commandin' officer, and he told her how much he liked him and admired him." She coughed slightly and I took the opportunity to take a breath.

"And I could tell you how that girl set her cap for that commandin' officer and married him. That wasn't bad for thirty-four years old, wouldn't you say? Considerin' she couldn't read till she was twenty-five?" Again, she didn't wait for an answer. "And I could tell you how she tried to be a good and loving wife, and how

184

she tried—and succeeded—in gaining the affection of her husband's children. I think I could tell you that." She paused and looked down at her hands, idle in her lap, then got up and started walking aimlessly about the room, touching objects tentatively as she spoke. "You'll be surprised, Mr. Brill, but all we wanted was to be normal. Not freaks. No one wants to be a freak. People want to be normal. So I worked at being normal. Perhaps I overdid it, I know"—she gestured vaguely at the carefully decorated room—"but I was overcompensating. That's what the doctor called it. Overcompensating for a deprived background. What do you think of that? Well, I don't care what you think." She took up a half-filled glass that looked like it contained Bourbon and drank it off. "You're just listenin', and I'm just tellin'.

"I'd like to explain about how the girl and her son tried to be normal after she got married, tried not to love each other any more. But I don't think I can. I don't think I can explain that they couldn't give each other up, however hard they tried. They didn't want to do what they did, but they couldn't live without each other —flowers and violins." She cut herself off, having heard her own voice, and looked at me from the General's desk, leaning slightly against the back of his chair. "Have you any idea the torture I went through when Tony went away? When he was captured? When I learned I might never see him again—the one person in the world who meant anything to me? Or can't you get past what we were, Mr. Brill? But when I found out he was alive, and when he came back to me, I knew that nothing, *nothing* would ever take him away again." Her green eyes gleamed briefly in triumph. "Course I thought it was all over." She took another pull at the dregs of her drink. "Only it wasn't."

"Mrs. Rollins—"

"I know, I know." Her smile remained, apparently frozen on her face. "Now it really *is* over. And it doesn't make any difference whether I can explain it or not. Over. And to you, I know, it's simply depraved"—she stretched out the word with a full Southern lilt, deliberately parodying herself, a jet-age Tennessee Williams heroine—"so why bother with explanations that no one would understand?"

"Will you come with me now, Mrs. Rollins?"

"Weah? 'Downtown'?" She giggled and her voice simpered to throaty life with a chuckle of flirtatious ante-bellum gaiety. "Will I come with you? No, I reckon, I won't just yet, if you all don't mind."

Her right hand emerged from behind her back with the gun from the desk drawer in it. She brought it up to her right temple before I could move.

"Now the fun begins." She was still smiling.